GERRY ANDERSON
& CHRISTOPHER...
**TERRAH...**

"DEEP BLUE Z"
WRITTEN BY
CHRIS THOMPSON

"ZERO'S METAL"
WRITTEN BY
ANDREW CLEMENTS

ARTIST
CONNOR FLANAGAN

ADDITIONAL ART
CHRIS THOMPSON

EDITOR
STEPHANIE BRIGGS

PRODUCED BY
JAMIE ANDERSON

# MARS INVADED!

### THE STORY SO FAR...

Mars has been overrun by a race of evil androids from the planet Guk! Led by Zelda, a 400-year-old witch with mystical powers to control matter, their fleet has destroyed humanity's Mars base and set up a beachhead to launch wave upon wave of devastating attacks against Earth.

Standing in their way is humanity's elite defence squadron, the Terrahawks, made up of five of the world's most talented pilots and a 200-strong army of spherical robots, the Zeroids. Based out of a top-secret South American base, this team uses their unique skills, resources and technology to combat Zelda's relentless attacks.

We join this story after almost a year of Earth being assaulted by the various horrors of the universe locked in Zelda's cryogenic store. Beginning to grow impatient with her ongoing losses, she plans her largest attack yet...

# EARTH ATTACKED!

# EARTH DEFENDED BY...

A child prodigy, genius engineer and amateur botanist. Hiro is the brains behind many of the Terrahawks' fantastic innovations, such as the memory data dump and the positronic brain of the Zeroids. Hiro commands Spacehawk, the Terrahawks' first line of defence against alien incursion.

## LT. HIRO

Hawkeye, the nickname of Hedley Howard Henderson the Third, is the Terrahawks' marksman and gunner of their atmospheric fighter Hawkwing. A keen athlete at a young age, Hawkeye was partially blinded in an accident and had to undergo an operation to restore his vision with experimental bionic eyes. His now augmented vision and skilled hand-eye coordination have made him one of the world's greatest marksmen.

## LT. HAWKEYE

## CAPT. KATE KESTREL

Few would believe that internationally famous pop star Kate Kestrel is actually one of the world's greatest fighter pilots. While Kate never intended to become a superstar, her exclusive celebrity persona is actually the perfect cover for her role as the pilot of Hawkwing.

Kate also has an extensive medical background which sometimes comes in useful when the Zeroid, Dr Kiljoy, is unavailable.

Astrophysist, pilot and second in command of the Terrahawks, Mary Falconer is an integral part of the team, piloting the Terrahawks' transport vehicle, Battlehawk, and countering Dr Ninestien's cold logical leadership with her more empathic approach. Mary has exhibited a degree of daredevil behaviour, however, and will generally be harder on herself than her team.

## CAPT. MARY FALCONER

## ZEROIDS

In an attempt to make the Terrahawks' operation more secret it was decided instead of recruiting a conventional fighting force, the Terrahawks would be equipped with an entirely robotic army. Two hundred spherical robots powered by a unique source - Iranium crystals harvested from the moons of Jupiter. These robots would be armed and equipped with a multitude of manipulator attachments to allow them to perform complicated tasks. The Iranium also allows the Zeroids to alter their mass enabling them to use their own kinetic energy as a weapon. In addition to Zeroids, Megazoids and Space Zeroids are used as the primary weapon on the Battletank and Spacehawk.

As what could possibly be a side effect of their unique power source, the Zeroids have started to exhibit individual personalities, deviating from their programming and exhibiting independent thought. This has clashed with Dr Ninestien's expectations of an organised fighting force , but for now the the Zeroids continue to develop as possibly humanity's first artificially sentient life form.

## DR. "TIGER" NINESTIEN

Ninestien is one of nine clones of the original Dr Stien, literally trained from birth to be a master tactician and leader of the Terrahawks. "Tiger" has proved time and again his wits when countering Zelda, combating her magic and mysticism with a cold, hard scientific approach.

In the event of his death, Tiger's memories and personalities can be implanted into one of his other eight clones ensuring the Terrahawks can not be deprived of their leader. This has left Tiger with a degree of self-loathing, like he's not really a full person.

Over the last year of commanding the Terrahawks, Tiger has become close to Mary, a situation he fears may cloud his judgement in command.

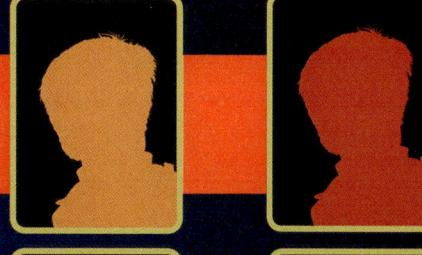

CHRIS THOMPSON

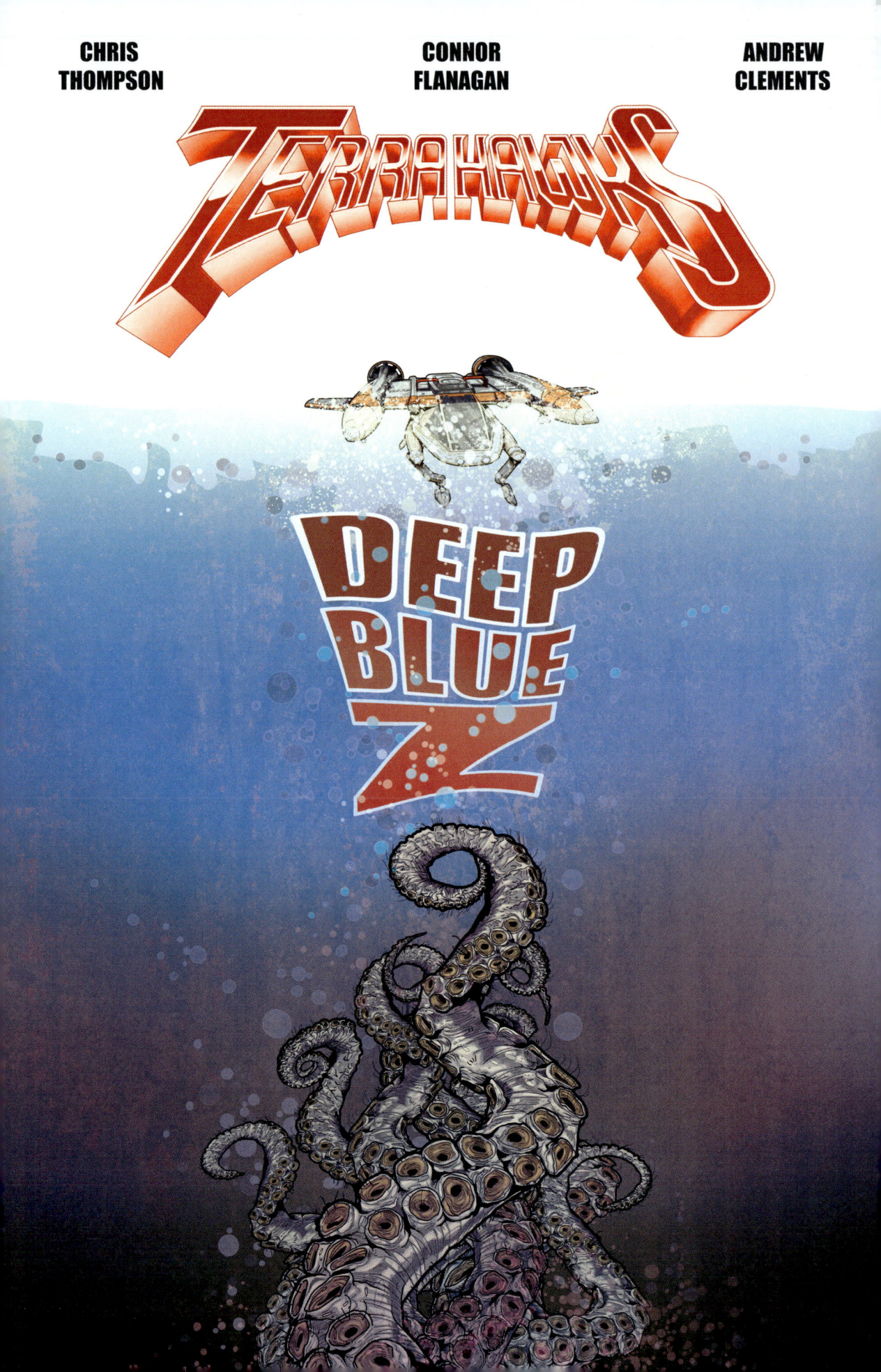

CONNOR FLANAGAN

ANDREW CLEMENTS

# TERRAHAWKS

# DEEP BLUE Z

STAY ON THIS CHANNEL...

LT HIRO!
EMERGENCY!
ZELDA EARTH ATMOSPHERE FIGHTER JUST APPEARED ON SENSORS, CLOSING FAST!
A DIRECT RUN?
THAT'S BASICALLY SUICIDE!
WE CAN'T TAKE ANY CHANCES.
DESTROY IT!
101
ORDERS SIR?

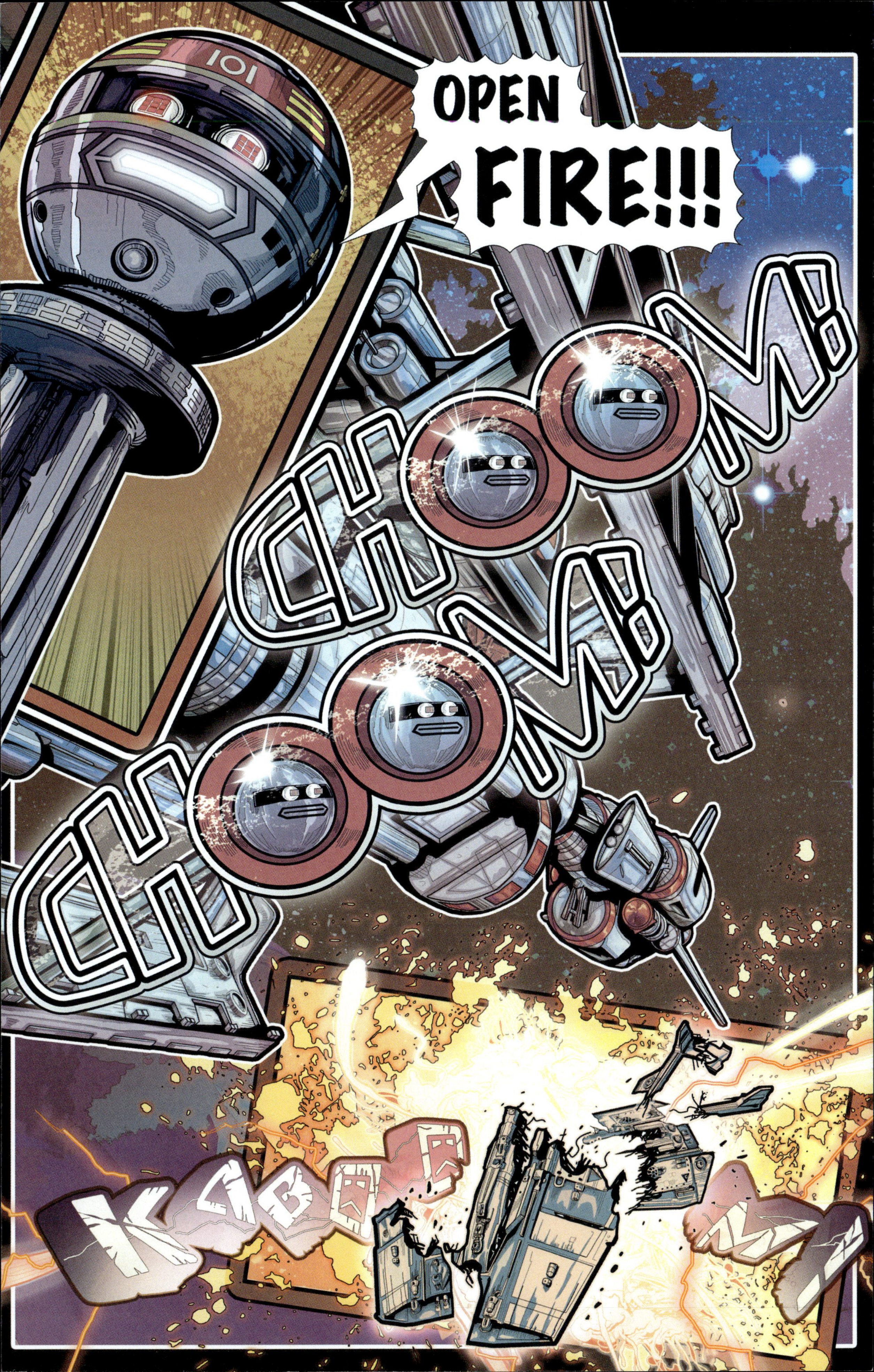
OPEN FIRE!!!
CHOOM!
CHOOM!
KABOOM!

TOTAL DESTRUCTION CONFIRMED!
GOOD SHOOTING 101!
SO... YOUR GRAND PLAN WAS TO DO THE EXACT SAME THING WE ALWAYS DO?
SILENCE CRETIN!
FOR ONCE THE ACCURSED TERRAHAWKS' BLASTED SPACECRAFT WILL NOT STAND IN OUR WAY.
BUT THE ZEAF MOTHER...
WATCH YOU FOOL!!
AND LEARN...

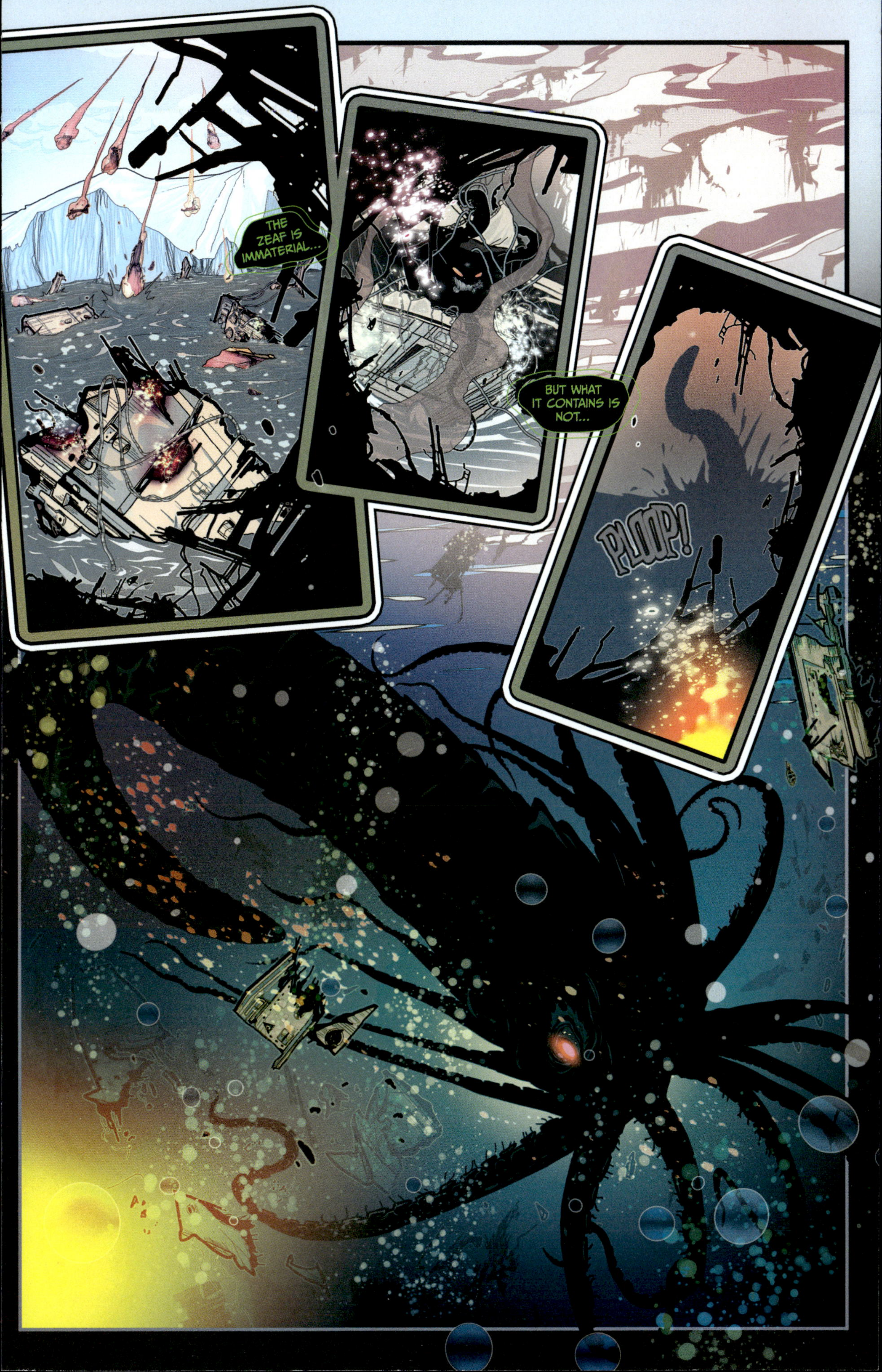
THE ZEAF IS IMMATERIAL...
BUT WHAT IT CONTAINS IS NOT...
PLOOP!

**VANISHED!?**

BZZZZZZZZZZ

MOWHAWK

IF IT WAS A SHIP I COULD UNDERSTAND BUT AN ENTIRE HYDROPONIC GREENHOUSE DOESN'T JUST DISAPPEAR.

NOT JUST ONE... THREE

INCOMING TRANSMISSION

WE'VE BEEN GETTING REPORTS FROM ALL OVER THE ARCTIC.

INITIALLY, IT WAS JUST THE ODD FISHING TRAWLER. NOTHING OUT OF THE ORDINARY, BUT NOW WHOLE STATIONS ARE BEING WIPED OFF THE FACE OF THE EARTH.

I NEED YOU UP THERE AND FAST. 30 PER CENT OF THE WORLD'S FOOD IS GROWN AT SEA. IF SOMETHING IS TARGETING THOSE STATIONS THEN WE COULD HAVE A GLOBAL DISASTER ON OUR HANDS.

UNDERSTOOD, WE'RE ON OUR WAY.

DO YOU THINK IT'S ZELDA?

ALMOST CERTAINLY. SHE MUST HAVE SLIPPED SOMETHING PAST OUR DEFENCES, AND NOW, WHATEVER IT IS, IT'S TARGETING EARTH'S FOOD PRODUCTION.

RECALL KATE! SHE'LL HAVE TO CATCH US UP.

**IMMEDIATE 10:50!**

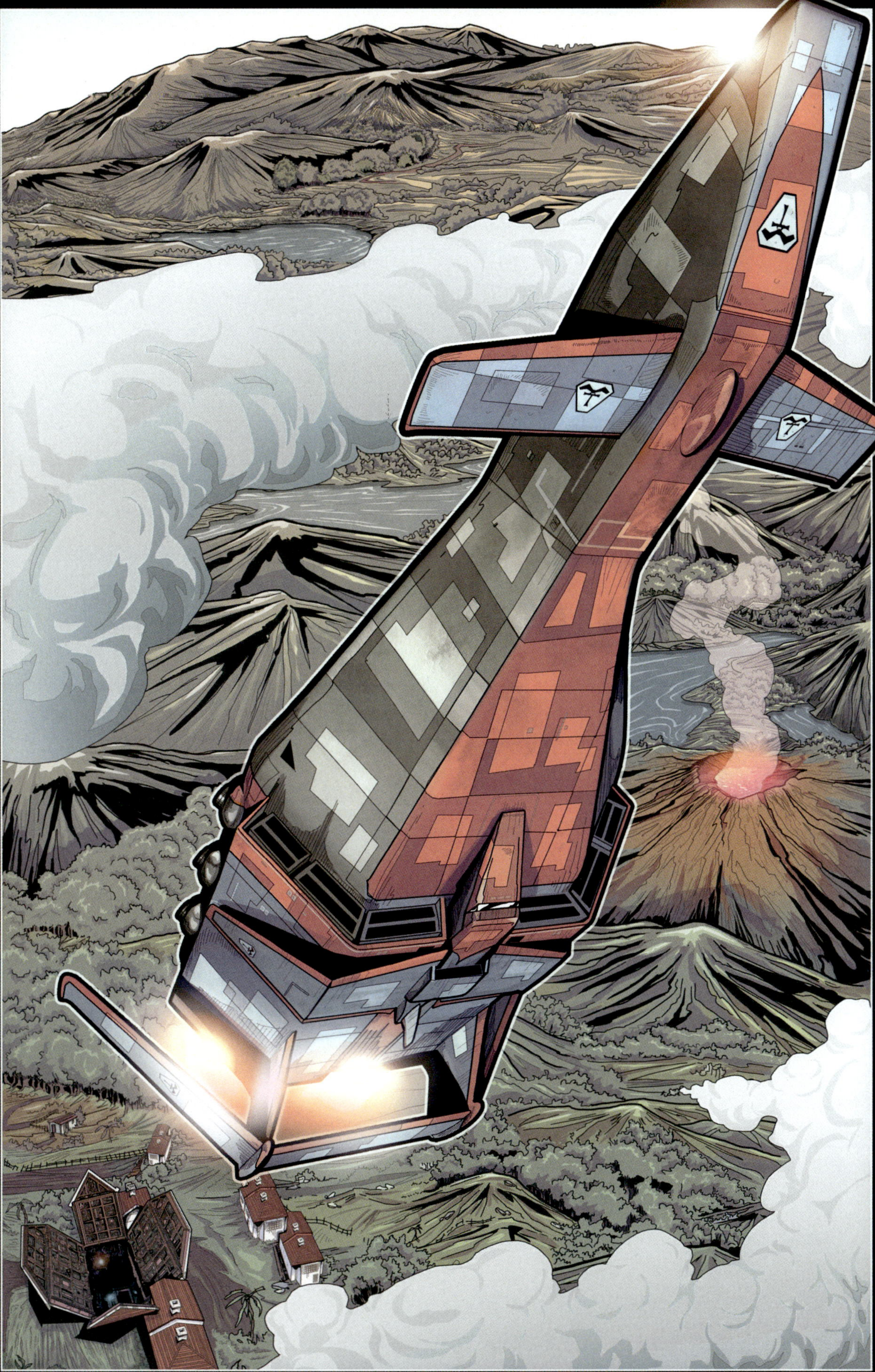

I'VE GOT WINGS SO I CAN FLY
FASTER WITH THE SPEED OF LOVE!
RECORDS
NR 1
WHEW!
WAS THAT THE ONE?
PLEASE TELL ME THAT WAS THE ONE!
THAT WAS, UM,
ABSOLUTELY
WELL PRETTY GROOVY,
AND LIKE TOTALLY RADICAL,
YOU KNOW MAN?!
GOTTA SAY, I DON'T KNOW HOW I FEEL ABOUT ALL THIS HOLOGRAM STUFF, I REALLY MISS THE ENERGY OF A LIVE AUDIENCE.
WELL IF YOU'D ACTUALLY COMMIT TO TURNING UP FOR A CONCERT...
WHAT WAS THAT STU?
NOTHING, MISS KESTREL!
THAT WAS PHENOMENAL KATE. YOU'RE GOING TO LIGHT UP THE HARPA MERIDIAN FESTIVAL! WE'RE GOING TO GET POST TO ADD ALL SORTS OF RAZZLE DAZZLE ON THAT!
LET'S DO SOME SHOTS FOR THE PRESS.
UH OH...

OH DEAR!
I'VE COME OVER ALL FUNKY.
IT... ERRR...
MUST BE THE FENG-SHUI IN THIS PLACE!
UM, THE FUN WHAT?
IT'S JUST INTOLERABLE! MY CHAKRAS ARE ALL OUT OF ALIGNMENT,
I'VE GOT TO SEE MY WELLNESS GURU AT ONCE!
BUT MISS KESTRAL!
WHAT ABOUT THOSE PRESS SHOTS!?
DO EM IN POST, HONEY!
WHAT'S APPENING STEW?
WELL MAN...
UH...
SHE JUST WALKED OUT...
LIKE...
AGAIN!
YOU KNOW, THIS WHOLE DIVA THING IS REALLY STARTING TO MAKE ME FEEL BAD FOR THOSE GUYS.
I'M SURE MR KING CAN CONSOLE HIMSELF IN THE...
*UGH*
GOLD PLATED LAMBORGHINI HE BOUGHT WITH THE MONEY FROM YOUR ILLUSTRIOUS RECORD CAREER.
NR 1
SO WHAT'S THE 10:20?
IT WOULD APPEAR THERE IS A SITUATION DEVELOPING IN THE ARCTIC.
BATTLEHAWK IS ALREADY EN ROUTE.
MR HENDERSON IS AIRBORNE AND READY TO RENDEZVOUS AT YOUR EARLIEST CONVENIENCE.
IN THAT CASE,
LET'S GO AND DON'T SPARE THE HORSEPOWER!

OVERFLYING THE TARGET AREA NOW.
ZERO, TAKE A TEAM OF ZEROIDS AND SURVEY THE SCENE.
SAH!
BOF!
UGH!
ARG!
SPLAT!
SPLAT!
SPLAT!
BRRRR
AT LEAST IT'S A SOFT LANDING.
ZUT ALORS, MY JOINTS ARE GOING TO FREEZE.
QUIET AS THE GRAVE...
TOO QUIET...

DOCTOR NINESTEIN, SAH!
NO SIGN OF HOSTILES OR THE HYDROPONICS DOME.
THERE IS A SMALL AMOUNT OF DEBRIS BUT OTHERWISE, THE PLACE SEEMS SAFE FOR LANDING.
WHAT DO YOU THINK TIGER?
I DON'T LIKE IT BUT I THINK WE NEED A CLOSER LOOK.
TAKE US DOWN ONTO THAT RIDGE.
RIGHT, LET'S GET TO THE BOTTOM OF THIS.

LETS GET THIS PARTY ROCKING CUZ HAWKWING'S ON THE SCENE!
10:10 KATE
ESTABLISH A TWO KILOMETER PERIMETER AND KEEP YOUR EYES OPEN.
THIS DOESN' MAKE SENSE.
NO BURN OR BLAST DAMAGE...
MOST OF THE DOME'S MASS HAS VANISHED AND WHAT'S LEFT HAS BEEN CRUSHED.
WE'VE SEEN THIS TYPE OF THING BEFORE - YURI, AND THE SPORILLA?
NOT ON THIS SCALE,
WHATEVER DID THIS WAS BIG ENOUGH TO GRAPPLE AN ENTIRE STRUCTURE AND PULL IT THROUGH THE ICE.
THIS DEBRIS MUST HAVE BEEN TRAPPED WHEN THE SURFACE REFROZE.
SAH!
I DON'T WISH TO ALARM YOU BUT THE GROUND APPEARS TO BE VIBRATING!
RUMBLE!

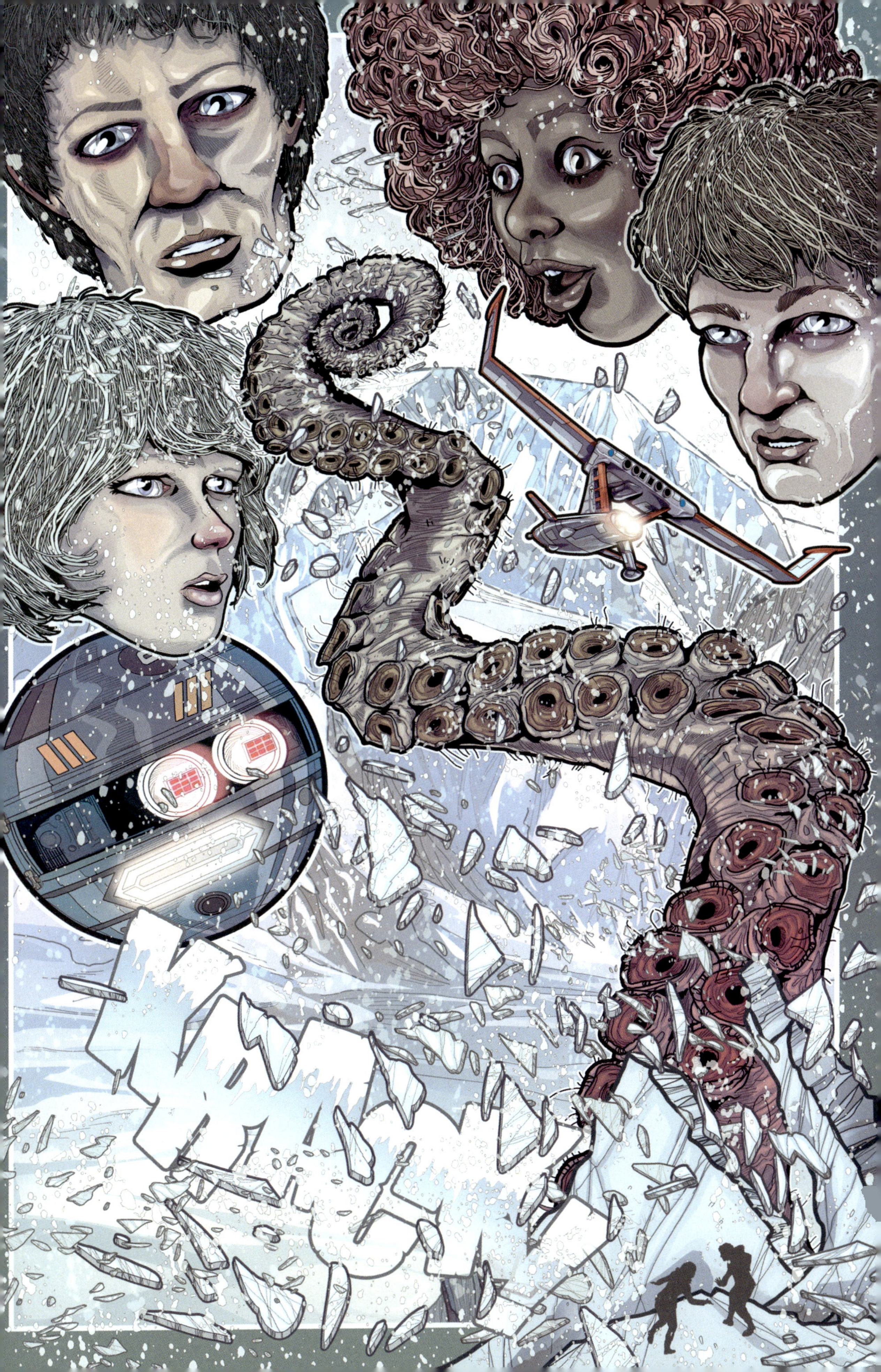

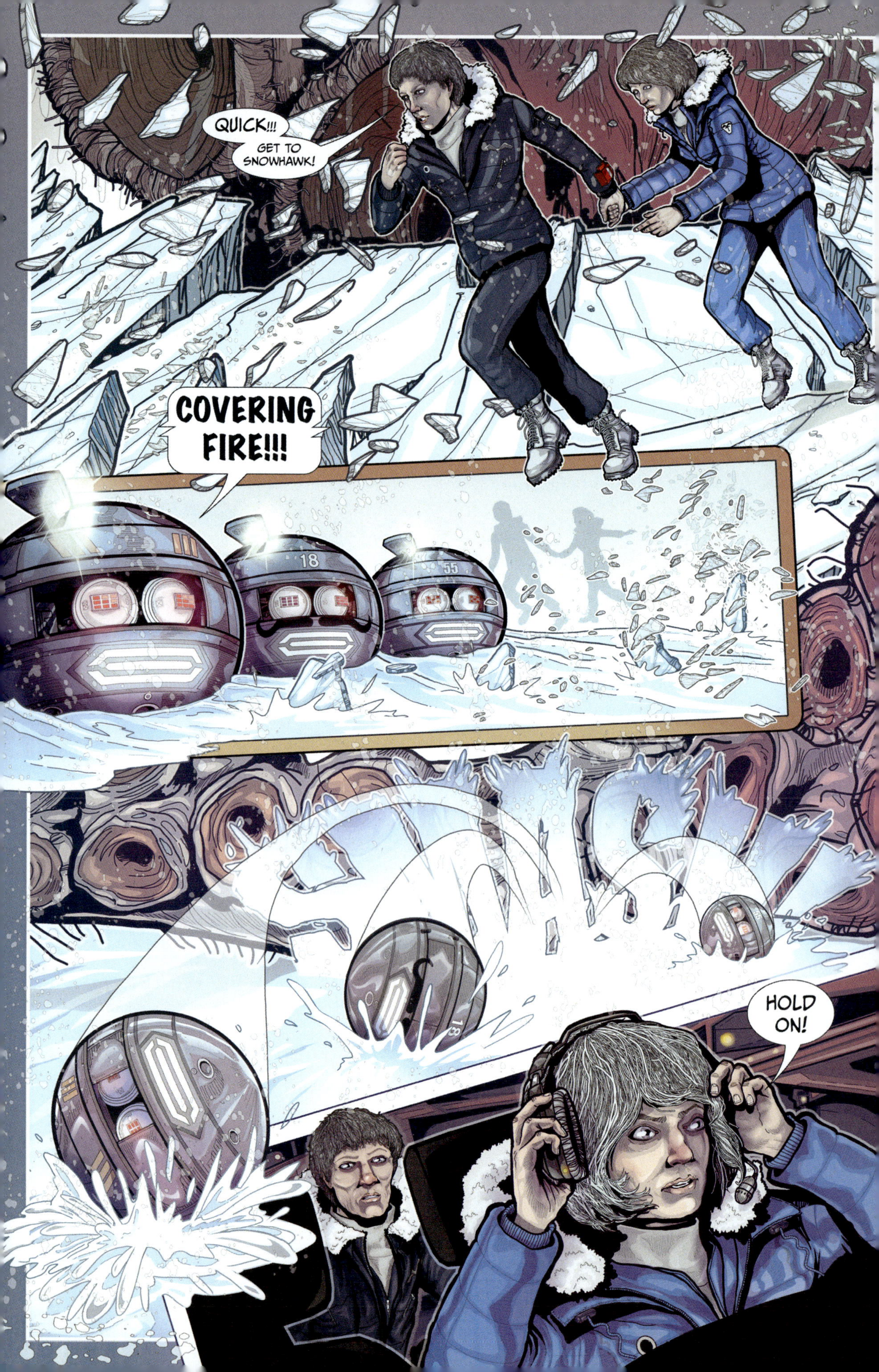
QUICK!!! GET TO SNOWHAWK!
COVERING FIRE!!!
18
55
HOLD ON!

VRRRRRM!
VRRRRRM!
CRUNCH
KATE!
COME IN FOR ATTACK!
10:10!
YOU READY HAWKEYE?
GET IT IN MY SIGHTS, KATE!

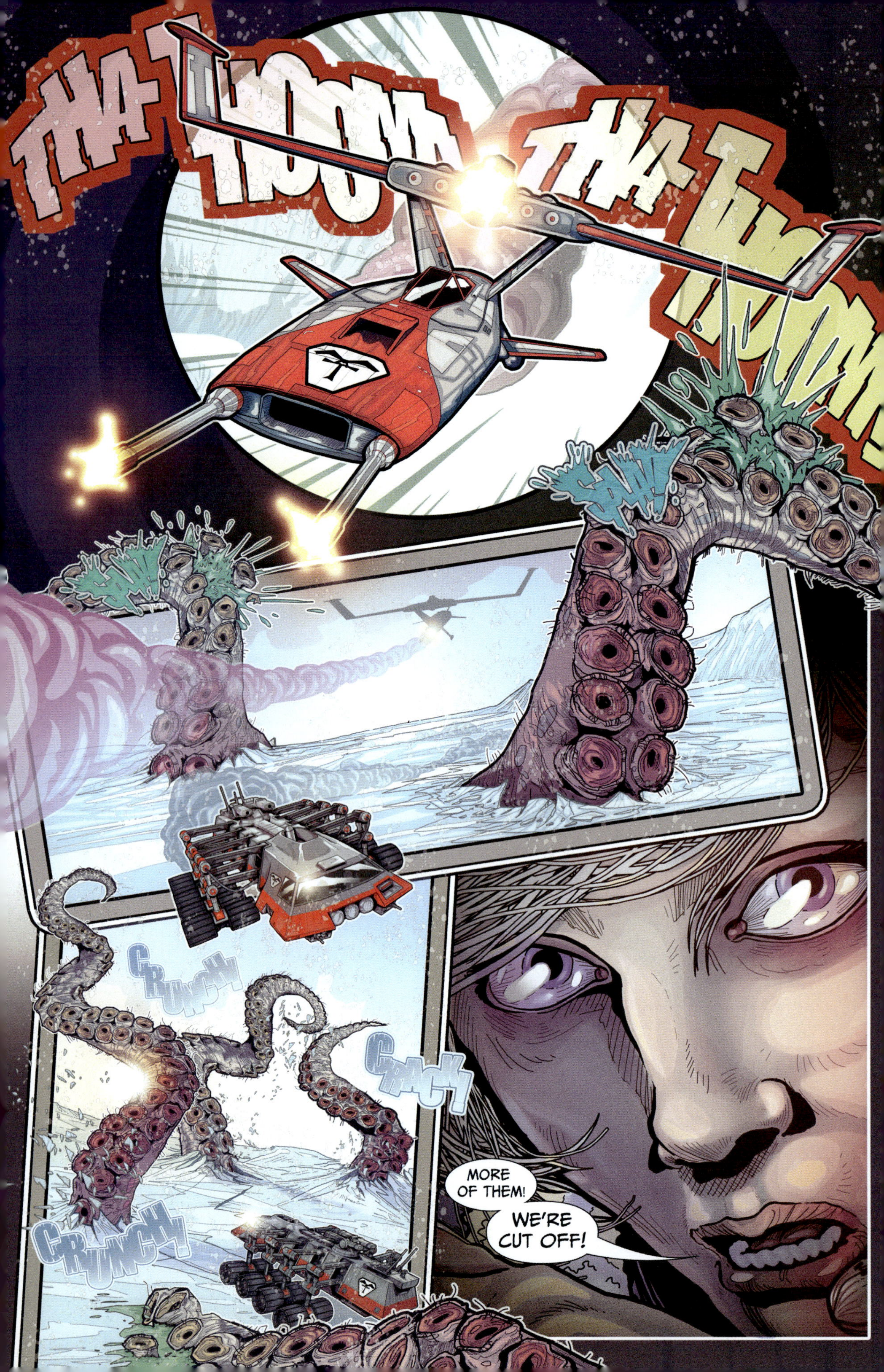
CRUNCH
CRACK!
CRUNCH!
MORE OF THEM!
WE'RE CUT OFF!

SHLK!!

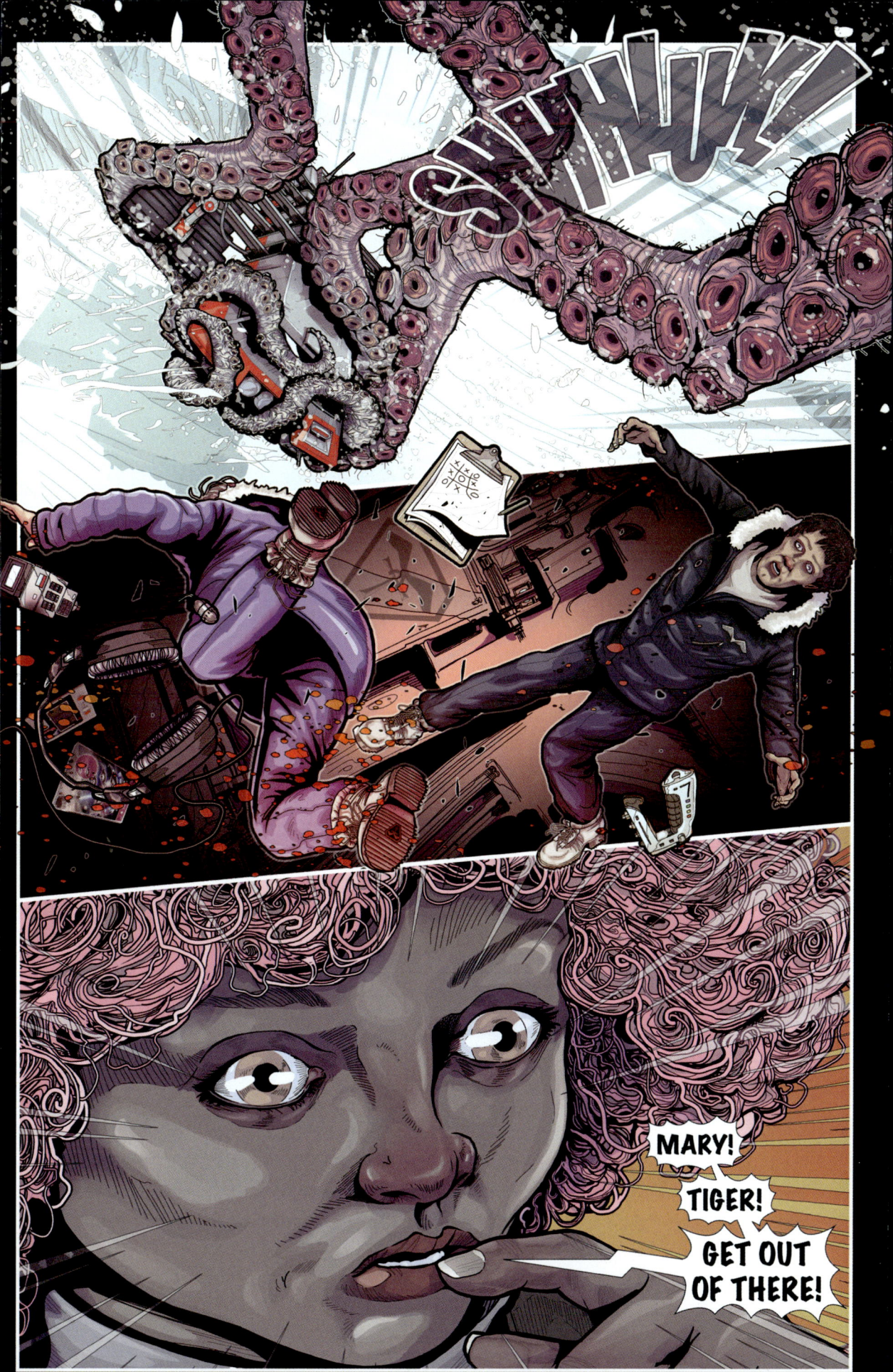

MARY! TIGER! GET OUT OF THERE!

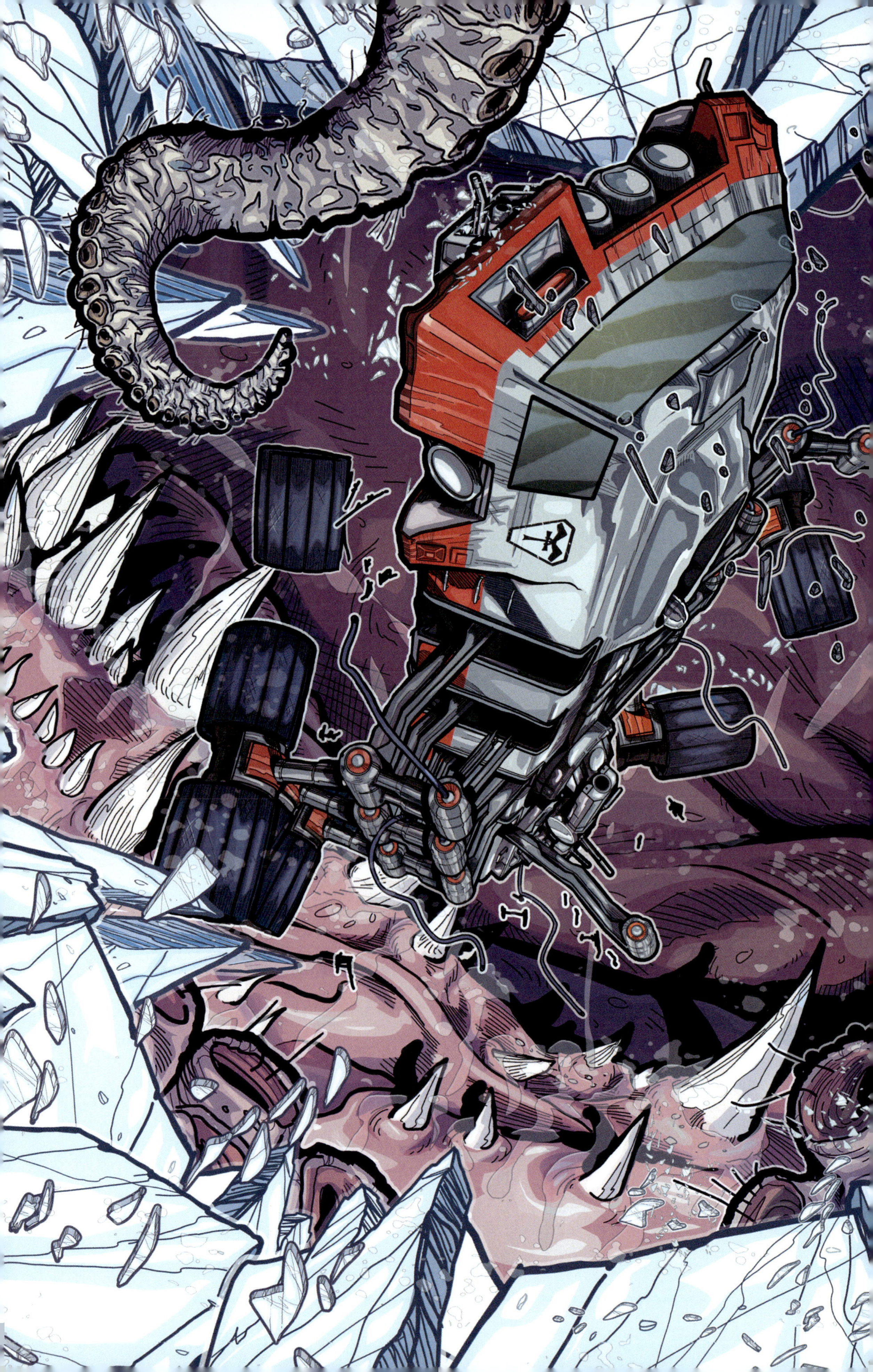

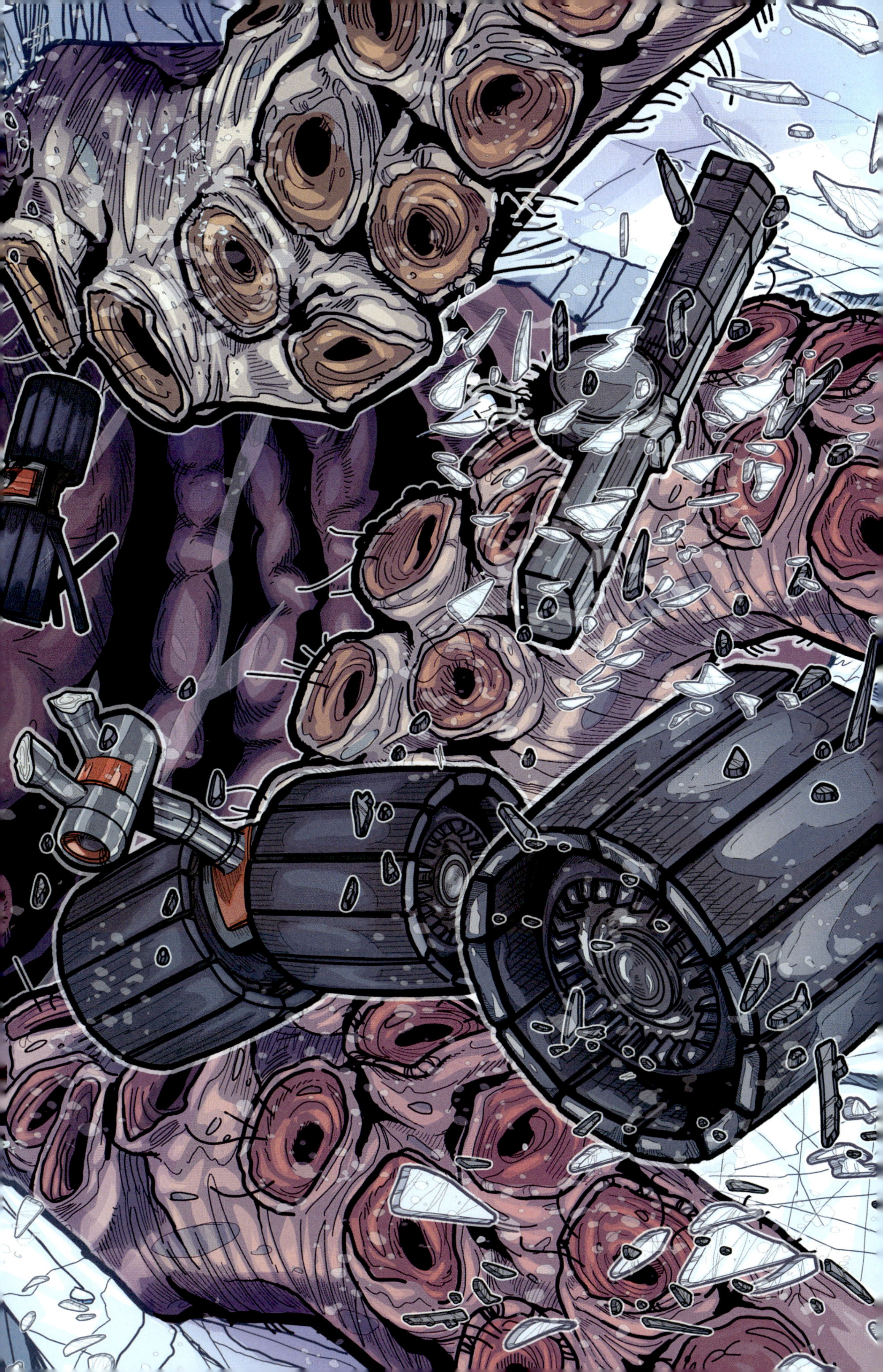

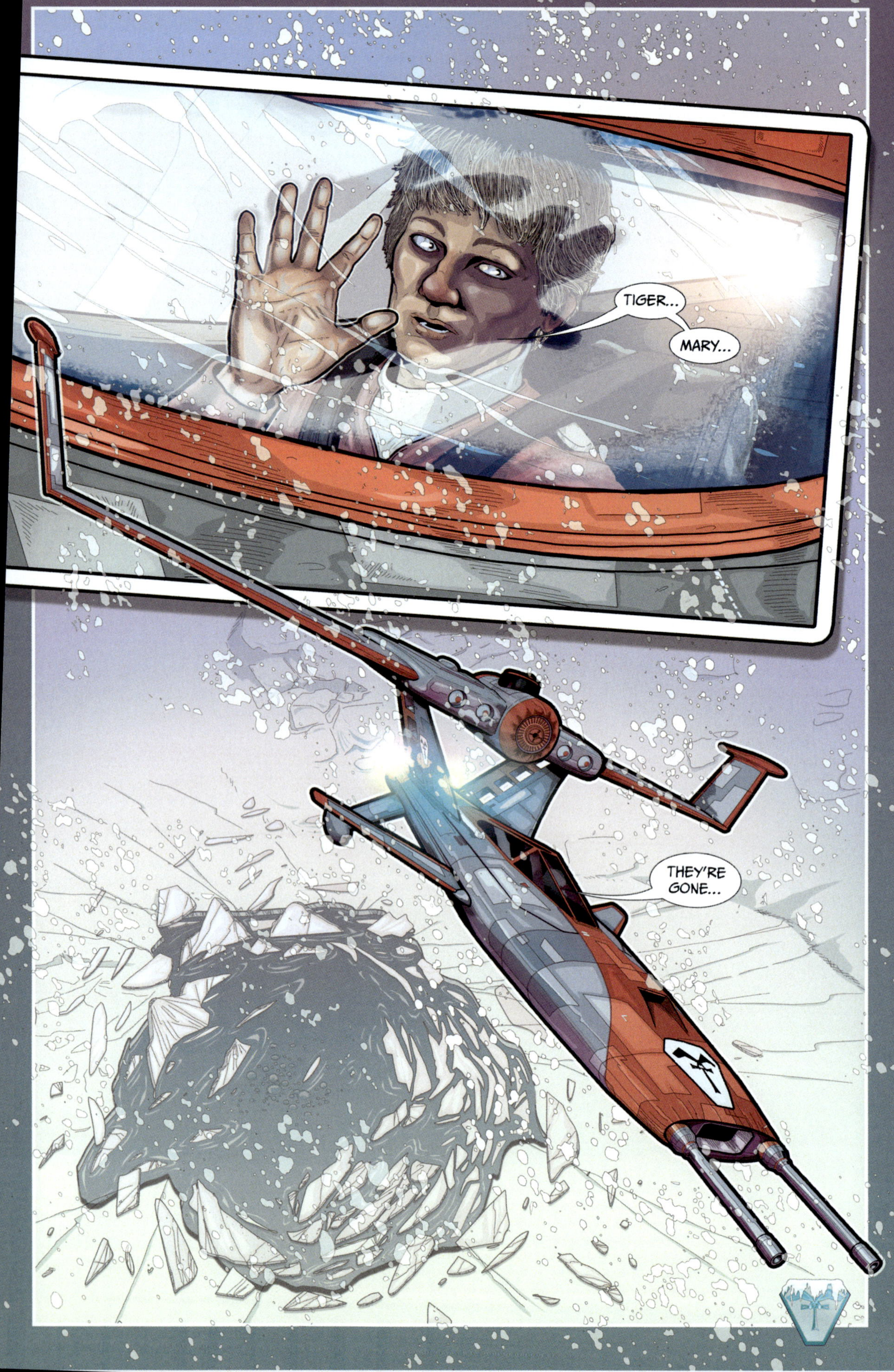
TIGER...
MARY...
THEY'RE GONE...

YOUNG TV ZONE
MAGAZINE
WEEK ENDING
31 DECEMBER 19
No.101 PRICE
LOOK OUT
IT'S ZELDA!
EXCLUSIVE
TERRAHAWKS
PICTURE STRIP!
PLUS
KATE KESTREL
ZEROIDS
AND SPECIAL EXCLUSIVE INTERVIEW
Kate Kestrel
THE SMASH HIT ALBUM!

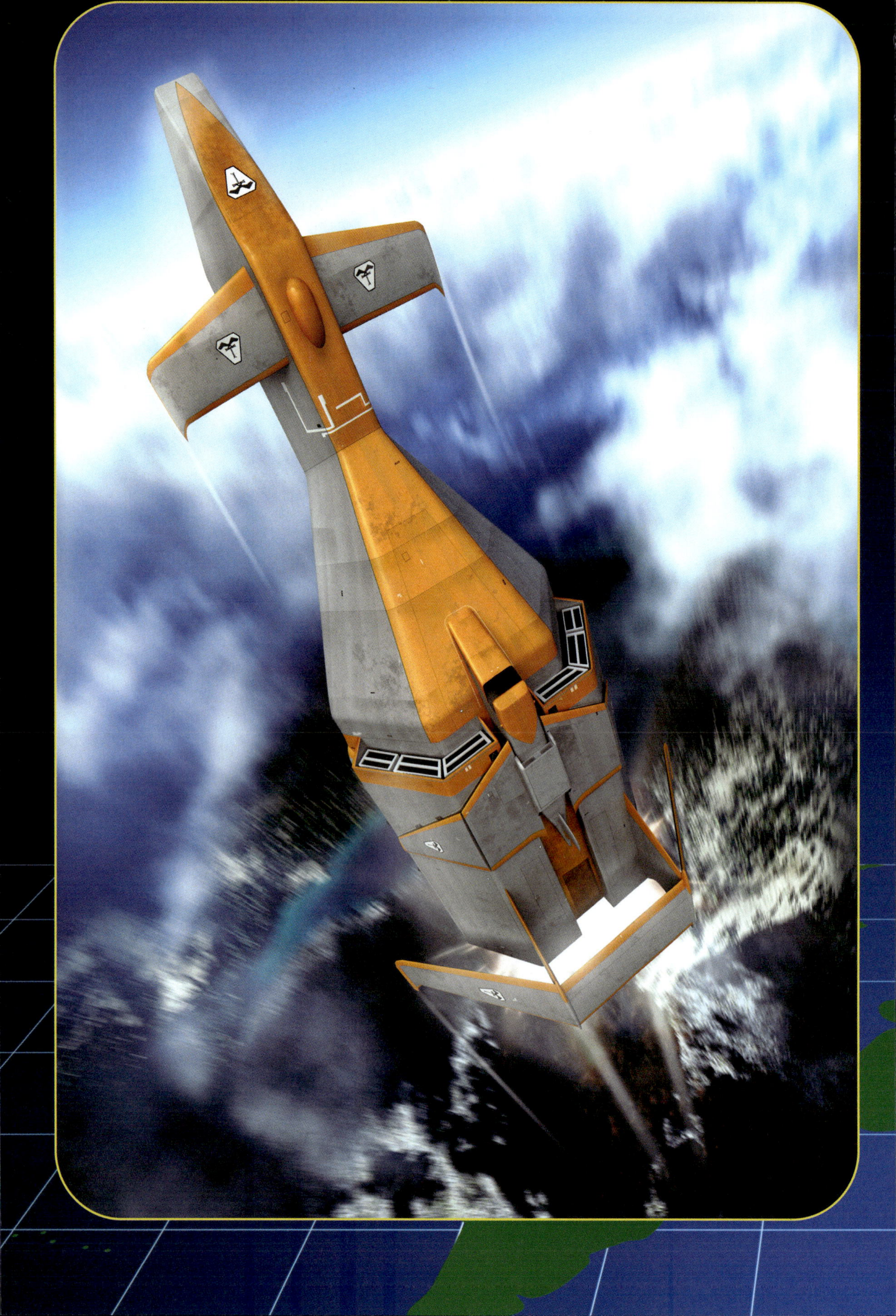

# BATTLEHAWK

The flagship, transporter and operational hub of the Terrahawks, Battlehawk is often at the spearhead of any of the Terrahawks' terrestrial operations. This gigantic aircraft sits at the centre of "Hawknest" and launches up through a vertical shaft, the top of which is disguised as a mansion.

The primary purpose of Battlehawk is to quickly move the Terrahawks' operational fighting force of Zeroids and combat vehicles to the scene of an extraterrestrial landing where it can quickly airdrop it's embarked forces via deployment tubes and its underslung hanger which either holds Battletank or Seahawk depending on the mission.

Once all its forces are deployed, Battlehawk will then pull back to a safe distance. If Dr Ninestien and Captain Falconer are required to oversee the battlefield then the primary flight deck can separate into its own vessel, the Terrahawk. This smaller craft is designed to perch on high vantage points or offer supplementary cover fire for Hawkwing.

For more specialised situations, Battlehawk can store other equipment in its aft cargo bay such as Groundhawk or Snowhawk. A forward cargo bay is accessible through the nose of the craft which also houses an excavator which can allow the vehicle to clear away debris to reach buried spacecraft. For this reason, Battlehawk has caterpillar tracks mounted to its landing gear allowing it to traverse terrain when landed.

# HAWKWING

Able to be fully armed and airborne within minutes of an alien incursion into the atmosphere, Hawkwing is the Terrahawks' hypersonic interceptor, designed to attack targets that may have been missed by Spacehawks defences.

Hawkwing is capable of reaching Mach 7.5 and is actually two integrated craft. The main control and drive section houses the cockpit and main flight systems while its detachable wing section, nicknamed Gunhawk, houses the primary engines, fuel and weapon systems as well as the gunner's cockpit.

In an extreme situation where Hawkwing is required to take on a much larger armed vessel, its gunning cockpit can transfer to the drive section and the remainder of Gunhawk can detach and act as a massive flying bomb. This does leave Hawkwing defenceless so it should be held in reserve as a last resort.

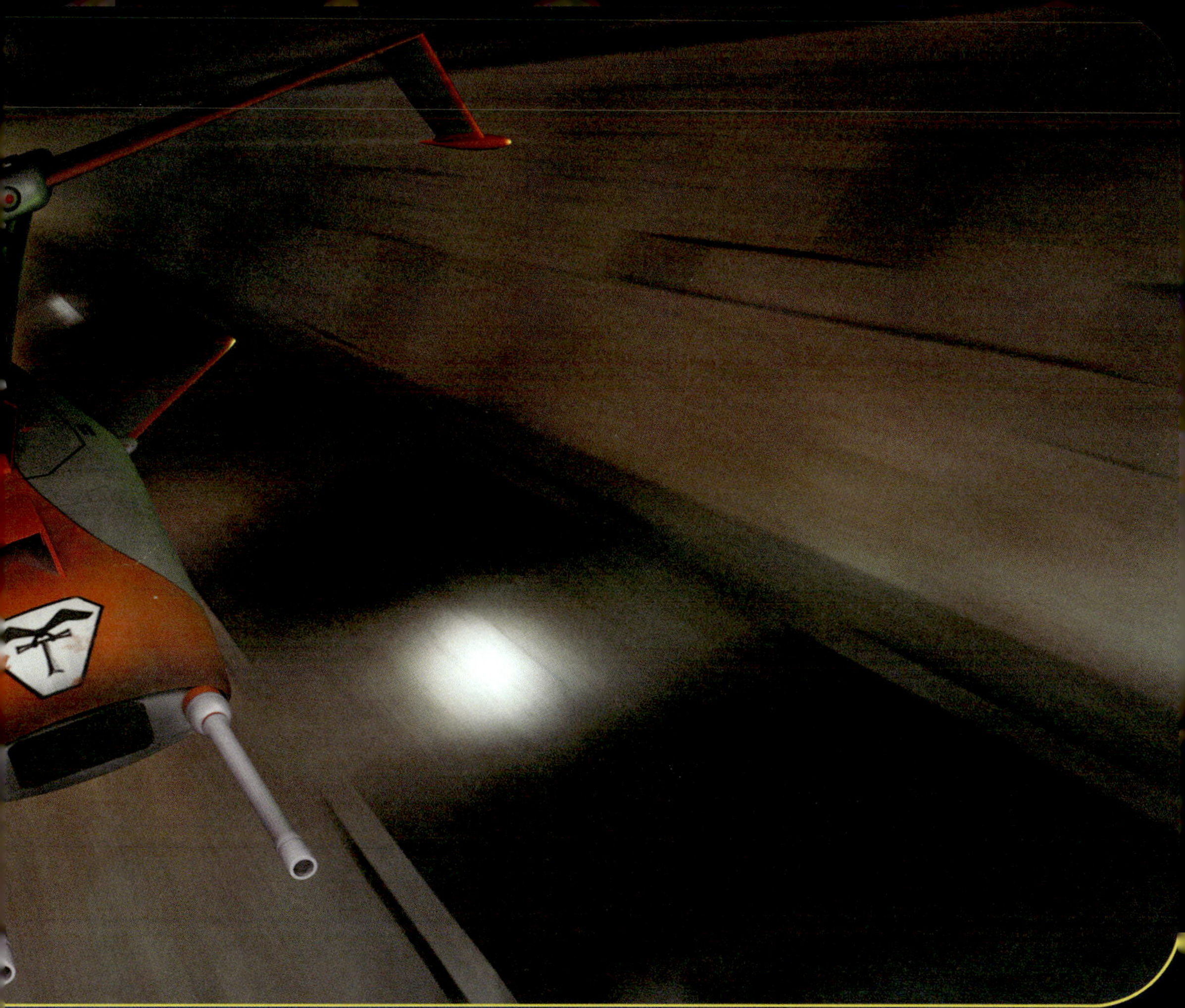

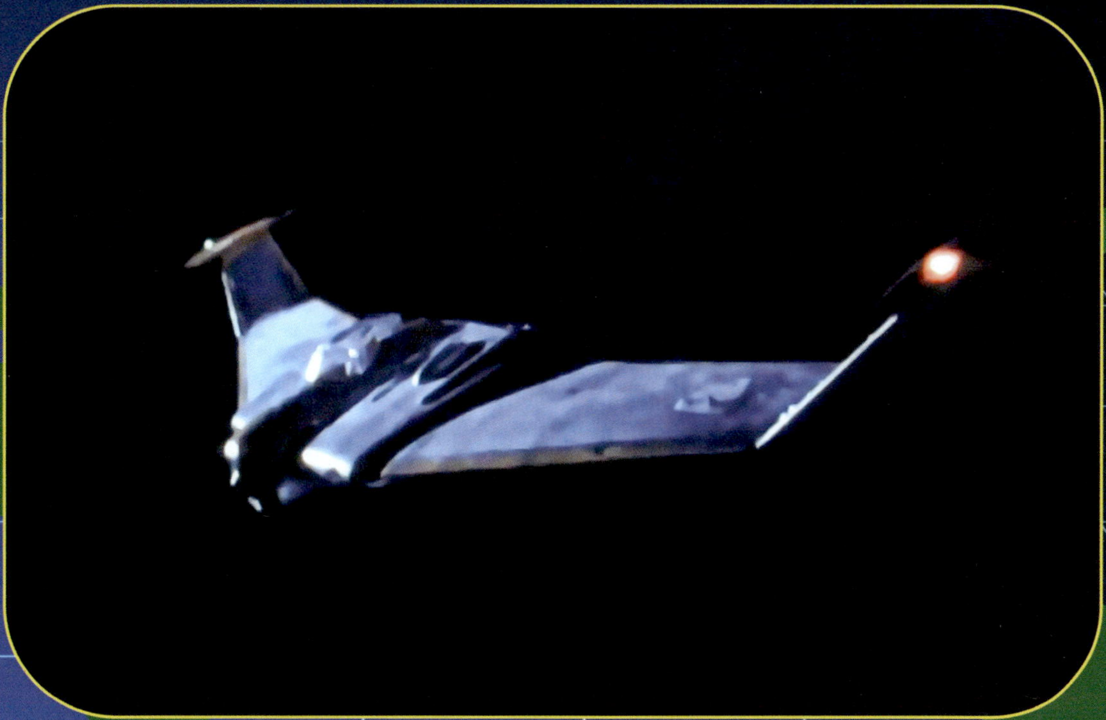

STAY ON THIS CHANNEL...

TIGER!!
MARY!!
CAN YOU HEAR ME!?
SENSORS CAN'T READ ANYTHING,
THEY'VE JUST GONE...
SOMETHING THAT ENORMÉ CAN'T HAVE JUST VANISHED!
WAIT!
QUIET LAD...
MISS KESTREL! I'M PICKING UP SNOWHAWK'S RESCUE BEACON!
SIGNAL IS STRONG BUT FADING FAST.
RIGHT!
THAT TELLS US THEY ARE, AT LEAST, ALIVE. DEPLOY SOME OF YOUR MEN TO TAIL THAT CREATURE AND BRING BATTLEHAWK BACK TO HAWKNEST.
WE NEED TO COME UP WITH A PLAN AND FAST.

IT'S CRUSHING THE HULL!

NO! IF I'M NOT MISTAKEN WE ARE BEING RAMMED DOWN THE CREATURE'S TRACHEA. IF I'M RIGHT WE SHOULD...

ARGH, ...STOP WHEN WE REACH THE STOMACH.

YOU MEAN WE'VE JUST BEEN EATEN?

I'M AFRAID IT'S STARTING TO LOOK THAT WAY.

COMMS SEEM TO BE OUT

ACID!

QUICK! WE'VE GOT TO GET INTO THE HAZARD SUITS BEFORE THE COMPARTMENT FLOODS.

I ACTIVATED THE RESCUE BEACON SO WE JUST NEED TO BUY TIME UNTIL THE OTHERS CAN GET TO US!

I KNOW WE'VE BEEN IN SOME DIRE SITUATIONS BEFORE BUT THIS TAKES THE BISCUIT.

NOT EXACTLY A DAY AT THE BEACH...

THERE'S NO POINT STAYING IN HERE, WE MIGHT AS WELL LOOK OUTSIDE.

IS THAT WISE?

PROBABLY NOT...

NO SIGNAL

FALCONER

NINESTEIN

NINESTEIN
FSSSSSSSH!
WELL...
I THINK THAT ANSWERS THE QUESTION AS TO WHERE THOSE DOMES WENT.

CONER
NINESTEIN
WELL...
WELL...
WELL...
WHEN I SENT THE GHARK TO EARTH, I REALLY JUST ANTICIPATED IT'D DESTROY SOME CROPS, STARVE SOME HUMAN VERMIN TO DEATH AND GET BLOWN TO SMITHEREENS WHEN YOU EVENTUALLY DID SOMETHING TIRESOMELY CLEVER TO STOP IT.
I WISH YOU COULD HAVE SEEN MY FACE WHEN I LOOKED INTO MY ICOSAHEDRON AND SAW YOU TWO...
COME TO GLOAT ZELDA?
OF COURSE NOT WENCH...
COME JOIN US!
AND CLONE, WE HAVEN'T HAD A PROPER NATTER SINCE THE ZYCLON.
FORGIVE MY FRIENDS...
THEY'VE NOT BEEN TOO CHATTY SINCE YOU FAILED TO SAVE THEM.
A SHAME,
THIS ONE HAD SUCH LOVELY HAIR...

NINESTEIN
YOU'RE WASTING YOUR TIME,
IF YOU WANT US TO BEG FOR OUR LIVES WE'D NEVER GIVE YOU THE SATISFACTION...
BELIEVE ME CLONE, WATCHING THE FLESH MELT FROM YOUR SKULL WHEN THOSE SUITS FAIL WILL BE IMMENSELY SATISFYING.
HOW LONG DO YOU HAVE?
TWO, MAYBE THREE HOURS?
AND IN FOUR THERE WILL BE ANOTHER NINESTEIN AND YOU'LL BE BACK TO SQUARE ONE.
THAT'S JUST IT!
YOU'LL BE BACK!!
BUT SHE WON'T!
I'M NOT DEAD YET HAG AND RIGHT NOW YOU ARE NOTHING MORE THAN A DISTRACTION.
WE'LL SEE HOW LONG YOUR RESOLVE HOLDS!
STAY HERE AND STEW FOR A BIT...
FALCONER
...AND I WILL RETURN WITH AN OFFER YOU CAN'T REFUSE!

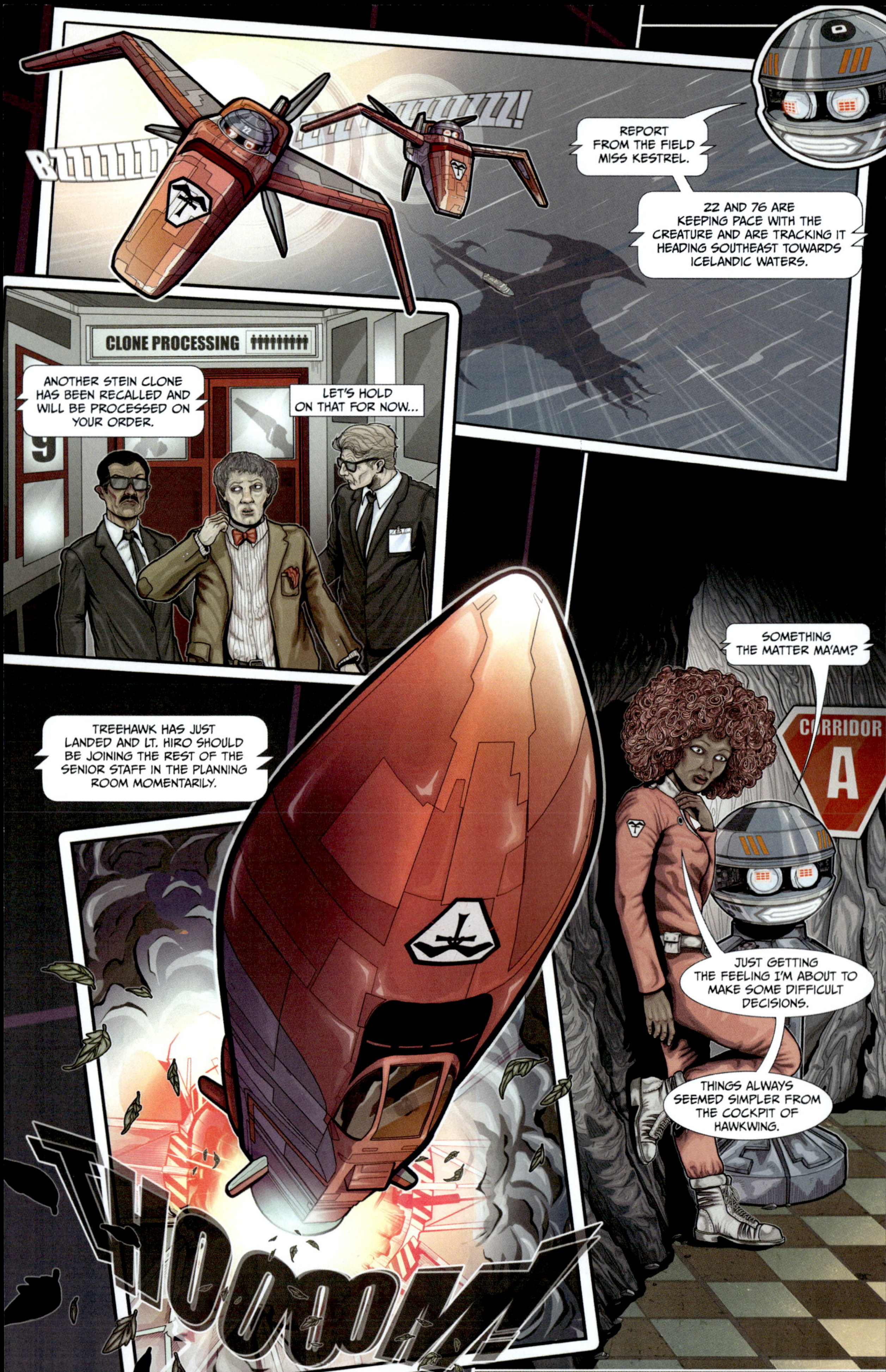
BZZZZZZZZZZZZZZZZZZZ!
REPORT FROM THE FIELD MISS KESTREL.
22 AND 76 ARE KEEPING PACE WITH THE CREATURE AND ARE TRACKING IT HEADING SOUTHEAST TOWARDS ICELANDIC WATERS.
CLONE PROCESSING
ANOTHER STEIN CLONE HAS BEEN RECALLED AND WILL BE PROCESSED ON YOUR ORDER.
LET'S HOLD ON THAT FOR NOW...
TREEHAWK HAS JUST LANDED AND LT. HIRO SHOULD BE JOINING THE REST OF THE SENIOR STAFF IN THE PLANNING ROOM MOMENTARILY.
THOOOOM!
SOMETHING THE MATTER MA'AM?
CORRIDOR A
JUST GETTING THE FEELING I'M ABOUT TO MAKE SOME DIFFICULT DECISIONS.
THINGS ALWAYS SEEMED SIMPLER FROM THE COCKPIT OF HAWKWING.

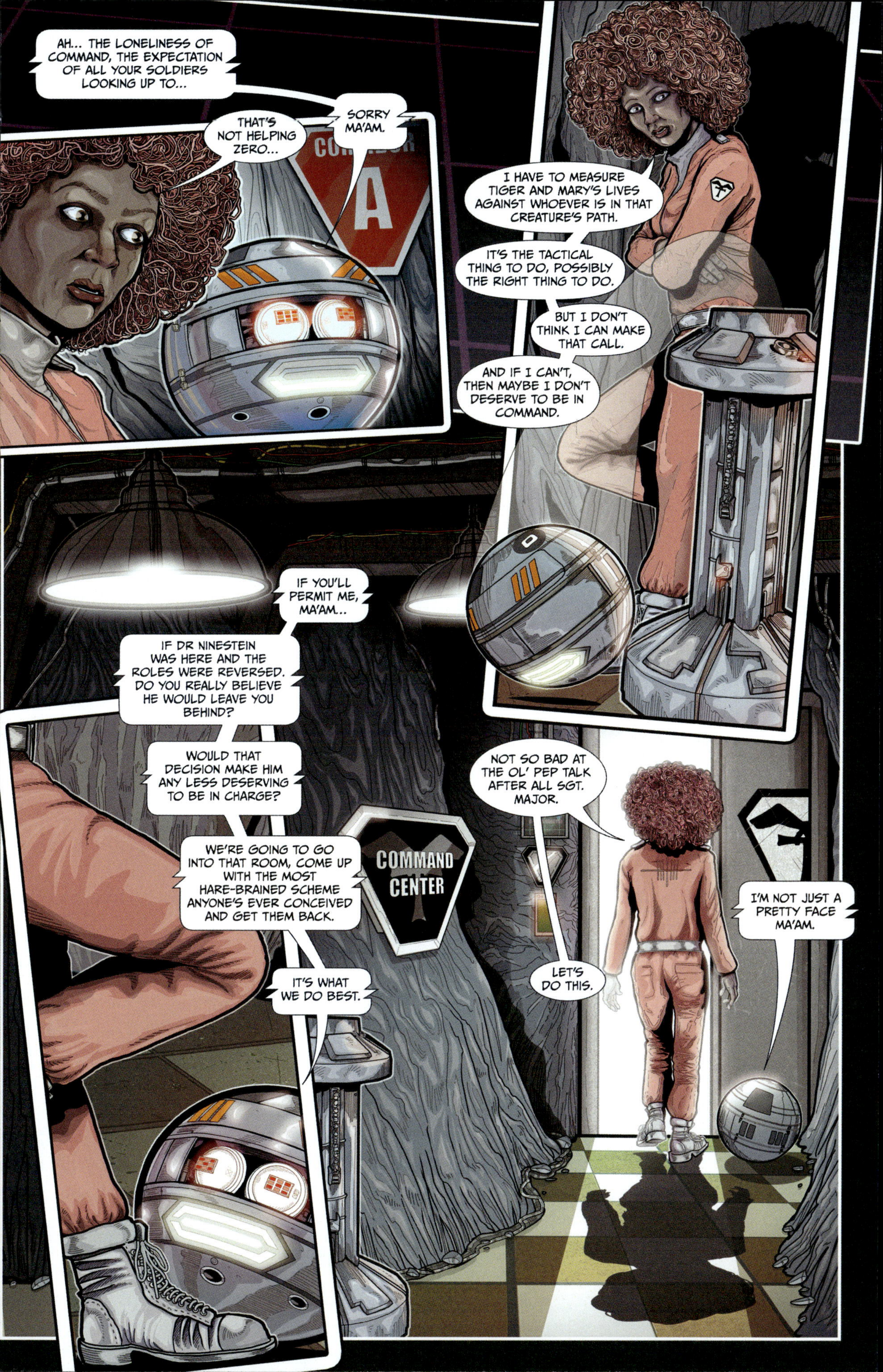

AH... THE LONELINESS OF COMMAND, THE EXPECTATION OF ALL YOUR SOLDIERS LOOKING UP TO...
THAT'S NOT HELPING ZERO...
SORRY MA'AM.
I HAVE TO MEASURE TIGER AND MARY'S LIVES AGAINST WHOEVER IS IN THAT CREATURE'S PATH.
IT'S THE TACTICAL THING TO DO, POSSIBLY THE RIGHT THING TO DO.
BUT I DON'T THINK I CAN MAKE THAT CALL.
AND IF I CAN'T, THEN MAYBE I DON'T DESERVE TO BE IN COMMAND.
IF YOU'LL PERMIT ME, MA'AM...
IF DR NINESTEIN WAS HERE AND THE ROLES WERE REVERSED. DO YOU REALLY BELIEVE HE WOULD LEAVE YOU BEHIND?
WOULD THAT DECISION MAKE HIM ANY LESS DESERVING TO BE IN CHARGE?
WE'RE GOING TO GO INTO THAT ROOM, COME UP WITH THE MOST HARE-BRAINED SCHEME ANYONE'S EVER CONCEIVED AND GET THEM BACK.
IT'S WHAT WE DO BEST.
COMMAND CENTER
NOT SO BAD AT THE OL' PEP TALK AFTER ALL SGT. MAJOR.
LET'S DO THIS.
I'M NOT JUST A PRETTY FACE MA'AM.

OKAY...
WHAT ARE OUR OPTIONS?
WELL...
AS WE THINK THIS CREATURE MUST HAVE ARRIVED ON THAT ZEAF THAT WE DESTROYED LAST MONTH, IT STANDS TO REASON OUR LASER WEAPONRY WILL BE INEFFECTIVE AGAINST ITS SKIN, EVEN SPACEHAWK'S.
925
WHAT ABOUT A BOMBING RUN WITH HAWKWING?
WHILE THAT MAY PROVE MORE EFFECTIVE, WE'D NEED IT TO SURFACE AGAIN AND EVEN THEN, THE BULK OF THE BLAST MAY JUST BOUNCE OFF THE CREATURE'S HIDE...
WHAT I'D SUGGEST IS THIS EXPERIMENTAL WARHEAD WE HAVE BEEN DEVELOPING IN RESPONSE TO MONSTERS SUCH AS THE SPACE CYCLOPS, THAT PROVED SIMILARLY RESISTANT TO OUR WEAPONRY.
A NOSECONE-MOUNTED DRILL THAT IS DESIGNED TO LATCH ON THE OUTER SKIN OF A CREATURE AND BURROW INSIDE, EXPLODING AND CAUSING MASSIVE INTERNAL DAMAGE.
WHILE MODIFYING IT ONTO OUR TORPEDOES WOULD BE A SIMPLE TASK, IT DOES POSE A PROBLEM...
AN EXPLOSION OF THAT SIZE WILL ALMOST CERTAINLY KILL TIGER AND MARY...

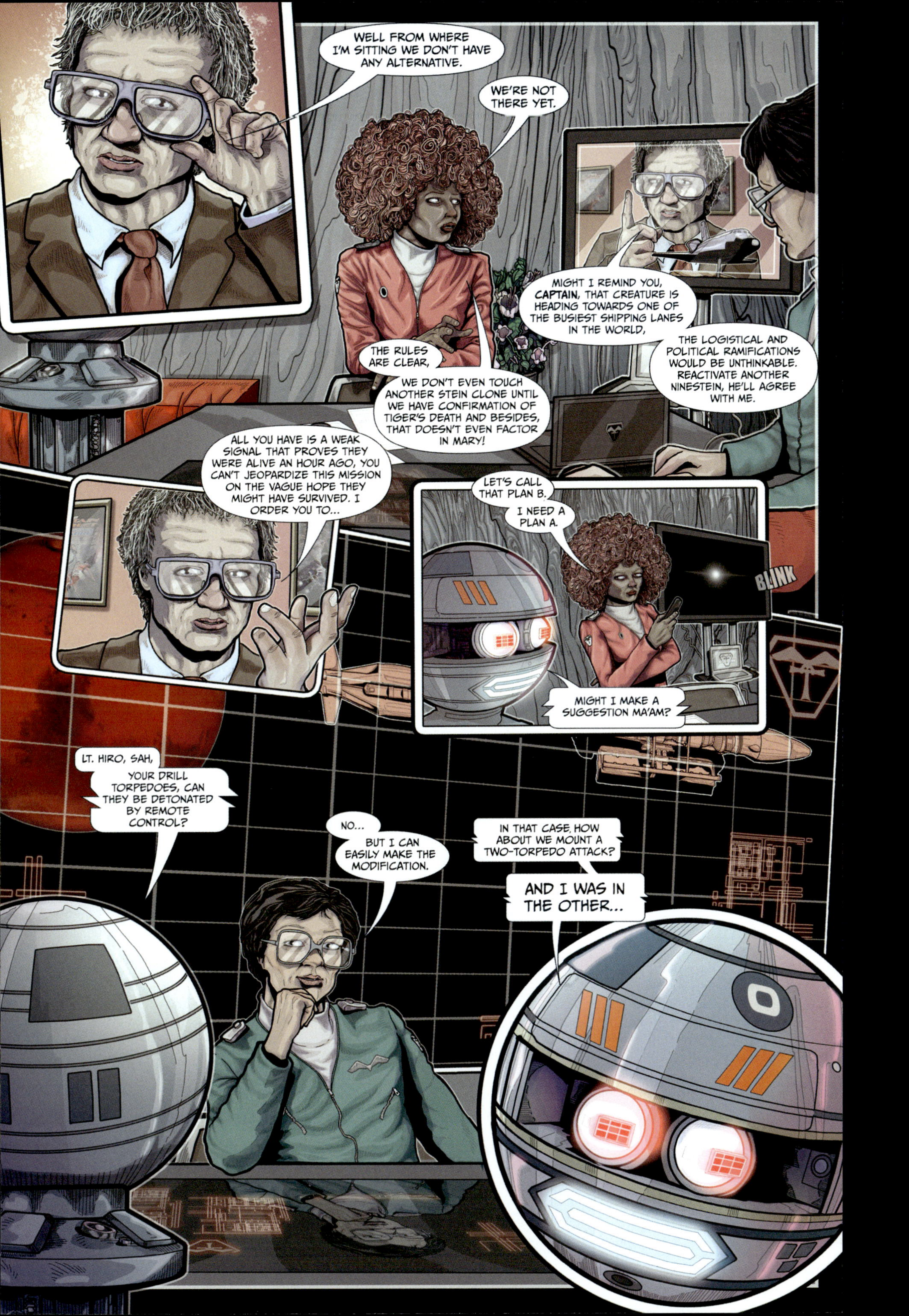
WELL FROM WHERE I'M SITTING WE DON'T HAVE ANY ALTERNATIVE.
WE'RE NOT THERE YET.
MIGHT I REMIND YOU, CAPTAIN, THAT CREATURE IS HEADING TOWARDS ONE OF THE BUSIEST SHIPPING LANES IN THE WORLD,
THE LOGISTICAL AND POLITICAL RAMIFICATIONS WOULD BE UNTHINKABLE. REACTIVATE ANOTHER NINESTEIN, HE'LL AGREE WITH ME.
THE RULES ARE CLEAR,
WE DON'T EVEN TOUCH ANOTHER STEIN CLONE UNTIL WE HAVE CONFIRMATION OF TIGER'S DEATH AND BESIDES, THAT DOESN'T EVEN FACTOR IN MARY!
ALL YOU HAVE IS A WEAK SIGNAL THAT PROVES THEY WERE ALIVE AN HOUR AGO, YOU CAN'T JEOPARDIZE THIS MISSION ON THE VAGUE HOPE THEY MIGHT HAVE SURVIVED. I ORDER YOU TO...
LET'S CALL THAT PLAN B.
I NEED A PLAN A.
BLINK
MIGHT I MAKE A SUGGESTION MA'AM?
LT. HIRO, SAH,
YOUR DRILL TORPEDOES, CAN THEY BE DETONATED BY REMOTE CONTROL?
NO...
BUT I CAN EASILY MAKE THE MODIFICATION.
IN THAT CASE, HOW ABOUT WE MOUNT A TWO-TORPEDO ATTACK?
AND I WAS IN THE OTHER...

NINESTEIN
UP HERE'S A BUST. FOUND ANYTHING?
AFRAID NOT.
I WAS THINKING, IF WE CAN FIND SOME SORT OF BURROWING OR CUTTING EQUIPMENT WE MIGHT BE ABLE TO GET OUT OF THE DIGESTIVE TRACT.
GOOD IDEA, A LITTLE MORE DIGNIFIED THAN THE OTHER ALTERNATIVE.
I'M GOING TO CHECK THIS WRECK OVER HERE.
HELLO CLONE!
WHAT DO YOU WANT?
I PROMISED YOU AN OFFER YOU COULDN'T REFUSE...
...AN OFFER TO SAVE YOUR DEAR BELOVED MARY.
NINESTEIN
I'M LISTENING.
IT WOULDN'T BE FOR FREE OF COURSE. I PROPOSE A TRADE...
CONTROLLING THIS BEAST IS TAKING UP A LOT OF MY POWER BUT I'D HAVE JUST ENOUGH JUICE LEFT TO EXCHANGE HER FOR ANOTHER ONE OF YOUR ACCURSED TERRAHAWKS.
AND WHY WOULD I DO THAT?

IN A FEW HOURS THERE WILL BE A NEW NINESTEIN, BECAUSE OF COURSE, THE WORLD NEEDS NINESTEIN.

BUT WHAT NO ONE REALISES IS THAT NINESTEIN NEEDS HIS FALCONER.

REMEMBER WHAT LIFE WAS LIKE BEFORE HER, THE COLD EMPTINESS, THE SINGLE MINDED PURPOSE YOU WERE BRED FOR?

THE REST OF YOUR TEAM ARE EXPENDABLE.

I WANT TO SEE THE PAIN IN THEIR EYES WHEN THEY REALISE YOU HAVE BETRAYED THEM. I WANT TO SEE THE GUILT ON YOUR FACE AS I FINALLY KNOW I CAN BREAK YOU.

THE NEXT YOU WON'T EVEN KNOW...

YOU CAN SPARE HIM THE GUILT...

JUST SAY YES!

NO!

I WILL NOT PLAY GOD WITH MY TEAM AND I WILL TAKE THE HAND I'M DEALT.

LOSING MARY WILL TEAR ME APART BUT BELIEVE ME, WHATEVER IS LEFT WILL COMPLETELY BE DEVOTED TO WIPING YOU OFF THE FACE OF THE UNIVERSE.

GUESS IT'S NO MORE "MR NICESTEIN" THEN?

SEE YOU IN THE NEXT LIFE CLONE!

YOU REALISE IF YOU HAD, I'D NEVER HAVE FORGIVEN YOU.
FALCONER
NINE
I BELIEVE THAT WAS THE POINT...
I WON'T PRETEND LIKE I WASN'T TEMPTED, BUT NONE OF US IS MORE IMPORTANT THAN THE OTHER,
WE'RE A TEAM.
FALCONER
NINESTEIN
EVEN THE SGT. MAJOR?
EVEN THE SGT. MAJOR.
FALCONER
NINESTEIN
WE'RE NOT GIVING UP THOUGH, RIGHT?
NEVER.

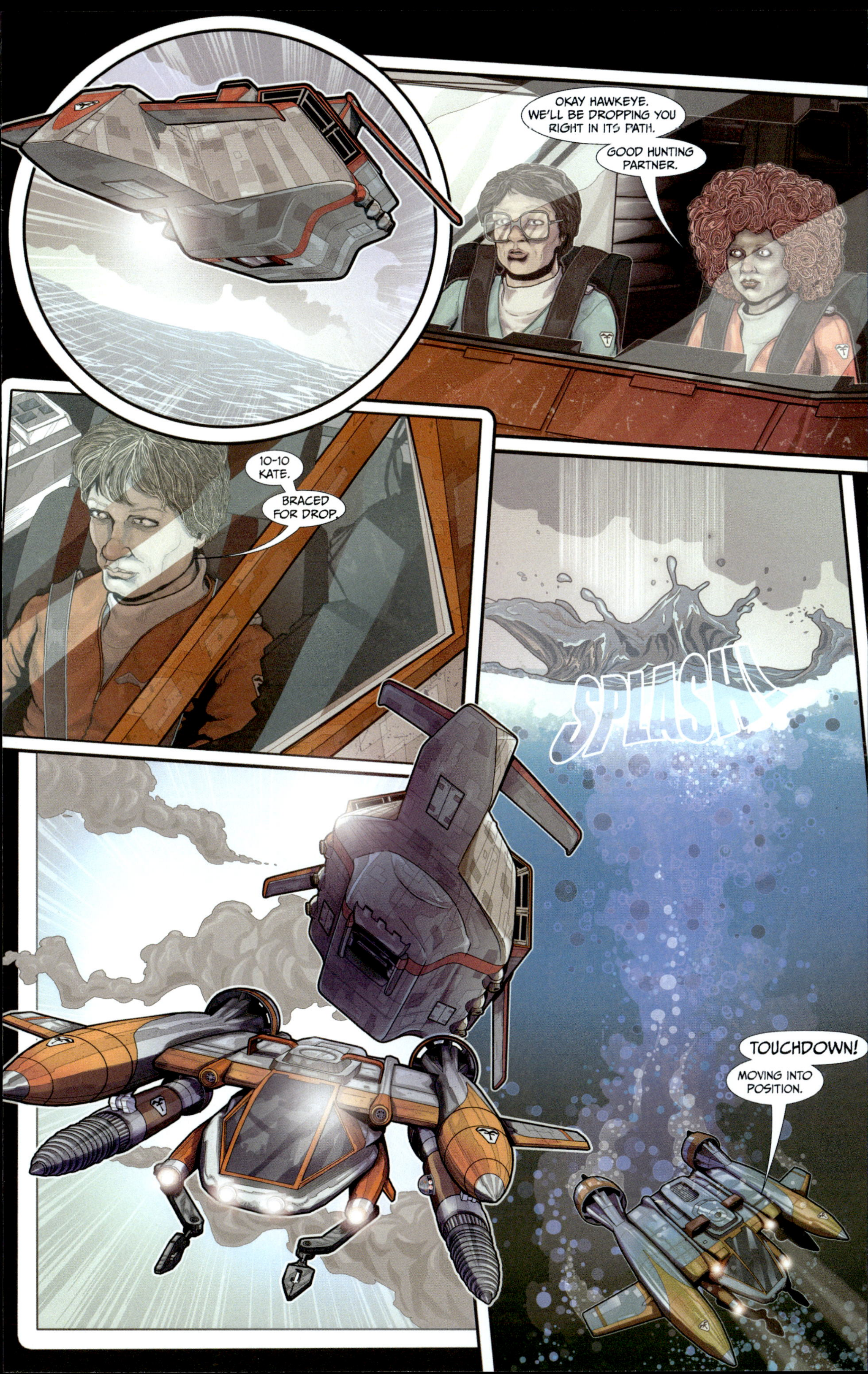
OKAY HAWKEYE. WE'LL BE DROPPING YOU RIGHT IN ITS PATH.
GOOD HUNTING PARTNER.
10-10 KATE.
BRACED FOR DROP.
SPLASH!
TOUCHDOWN!
MOVING INTO POSITION.

I'M GETTING A FAINT IMPRESSION ON THE SONAR.
IT'S NOT GOING TO BE ENOUGH FOR AN ACCURATE SHOT. I'M GOING TO HAVE TO WAIT UNTIL THE CREATURE COMES INTO VISUAL RANGE AND DO IT BY EYE.
HOW CLOSE DOES THAT HAVE TO BE?
CLOSE...
POINT BLANK RANGE...
HOLD YOUR NERVE SAH,
WAIT TILL YOU SEE THE WHITES OF ITS EYES.
I'M TRYING TO FOCUS ZERO...
SORRY SAH!
YOU ARE GOING ON ONE THE WARHEAD IS GOING ON TWO
YOU COPY?
10:10!

"300 METRES..."

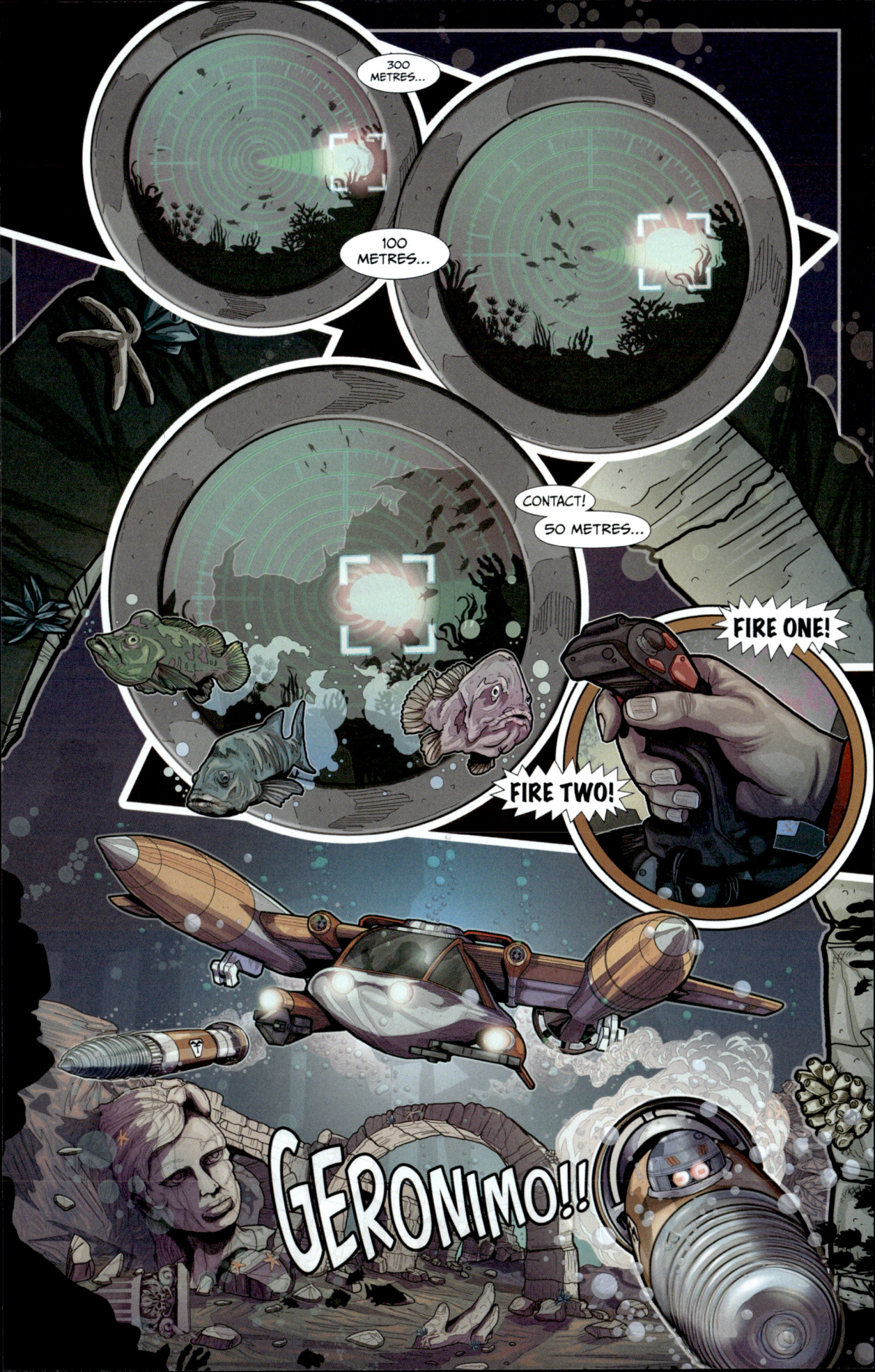

"100 METRES..."

"CONTACT! 50 METRES..."

"FIRE ONE!"

"FIRE TWO!"

GERONIMO!!

DIRECT HIT WITH ZERO BUT THE WARHEAD HAS GONE WIDE!
WELL...
THAT'S GOT ITS ATTENTION.

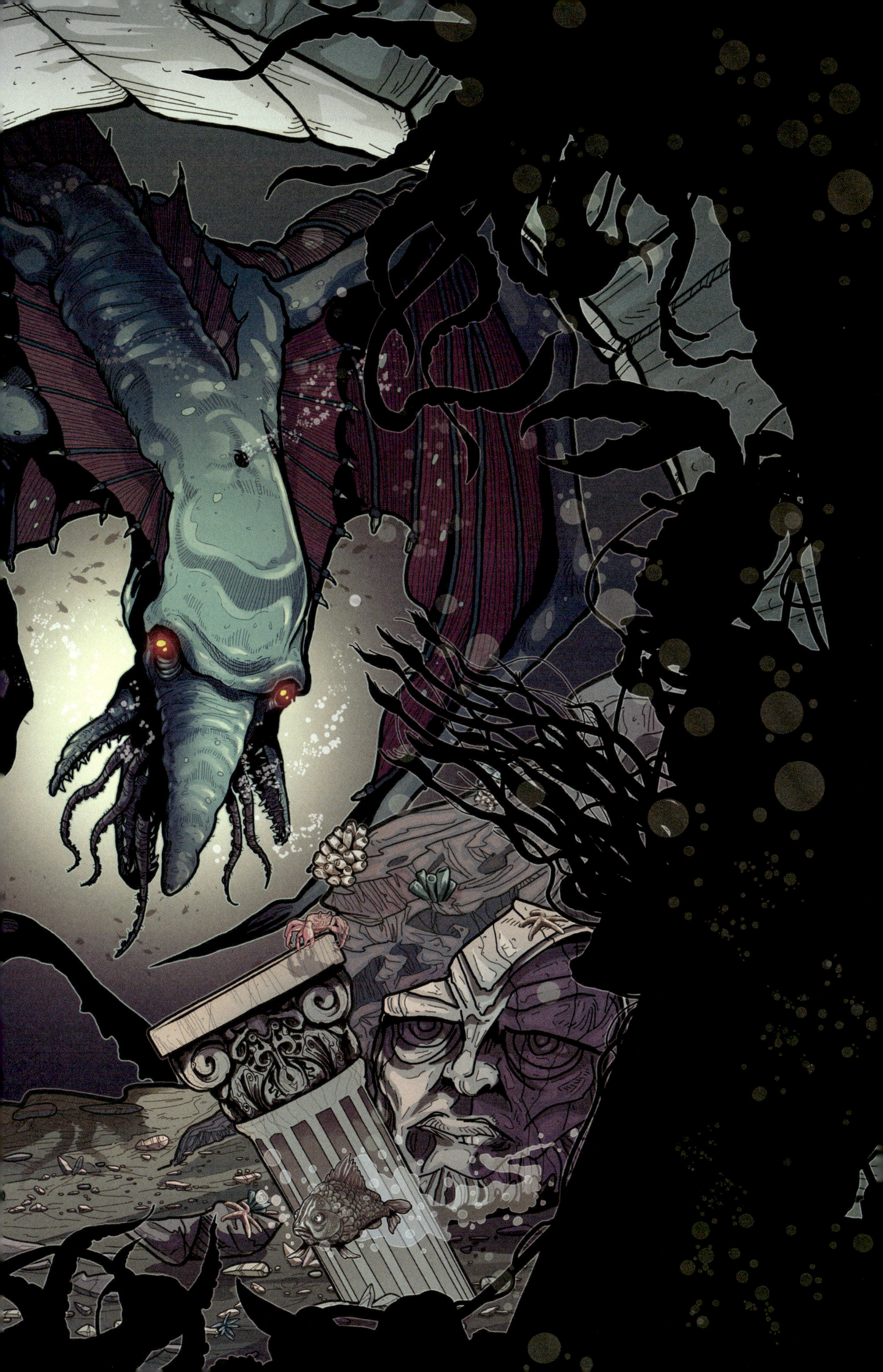

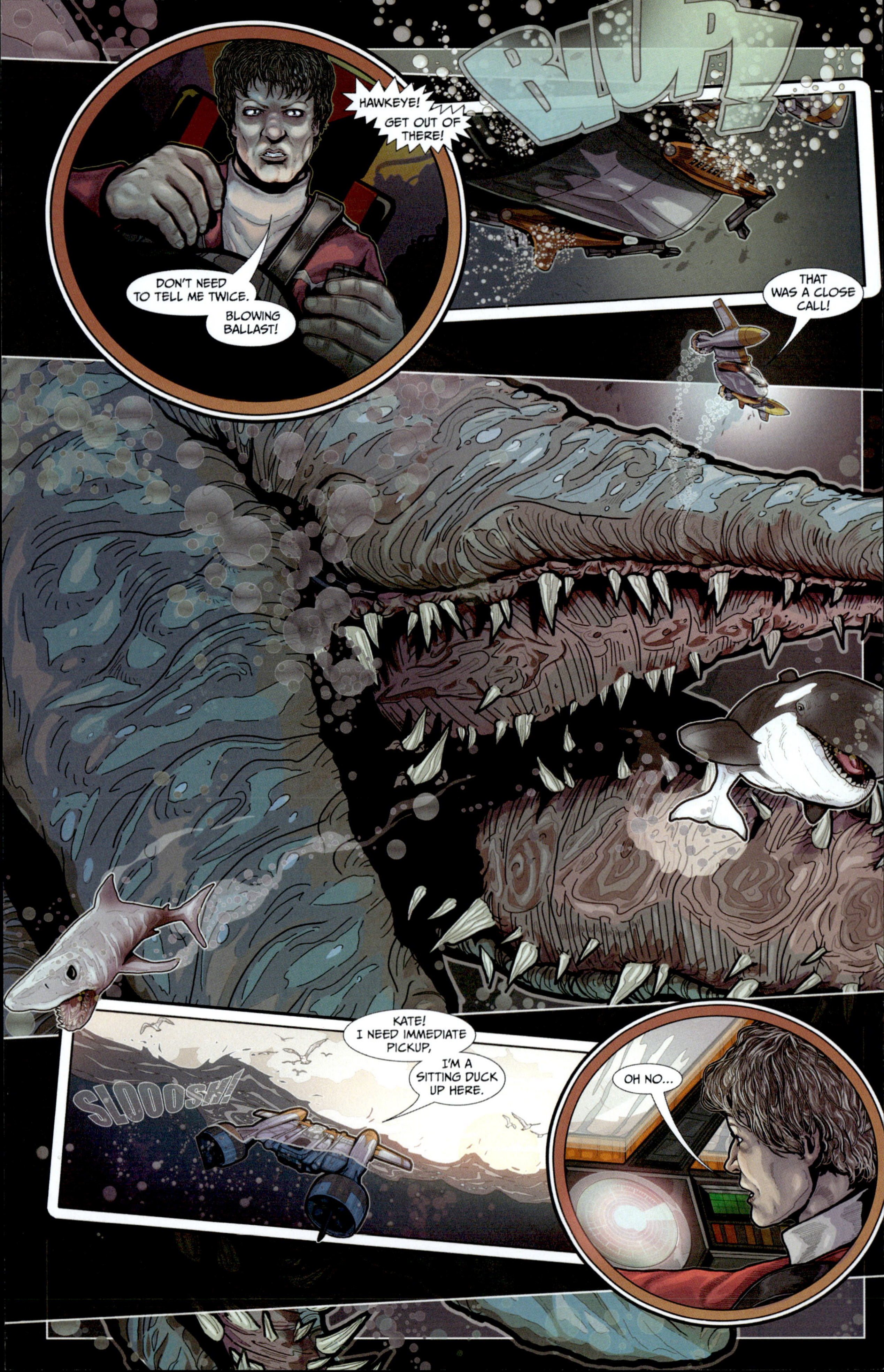

BLUP!
HAWKEYE! GET OUT OF THERE!
DON'T NEED TO TELL ME TWICE.
BLOWING BALLAST!
THAT WAS A CLOSE CALL!
KATE! I NEED IMMEDIATE PICKUP,
I'M A SITTING DUCK UP HERE.
SLOOOSH!
OH NO...

KATE!

KAATE!!?

Dwarfing anything else in the Terrahawks' fleet is Spacehawk, their advanced orbital Battleship and the first line of defence of Earth. This gargantuan vessel was designed in response to the failures of Earth's defences during previous alien invasion attempts. Rather than building a series of small satellites that are limited in range and firepower, a single vessel with weapons powerful enough to decimate anything from a small space fighter to a large meteorite was deemed the most efficient way to deal with approaching threats.

At over 500 metres long, Spacehawk houses a crew of 100 Zeroids, operating and maintaining the vessel, and banks of augmented Megazoids controlling the craft's primary weapons all of whom report to Space Sgt. 101 who acts as the primary interface between any human crew and the ship.

Spacehawk is also equipped with a series of deployable space vehicles including the MEV and Space tank, deployable rovers able to traverse planetary terrain, Hawklet - a small shuttle and repair pod, and Tomahawk - an experimental space fighter.

# SPACEHAWK

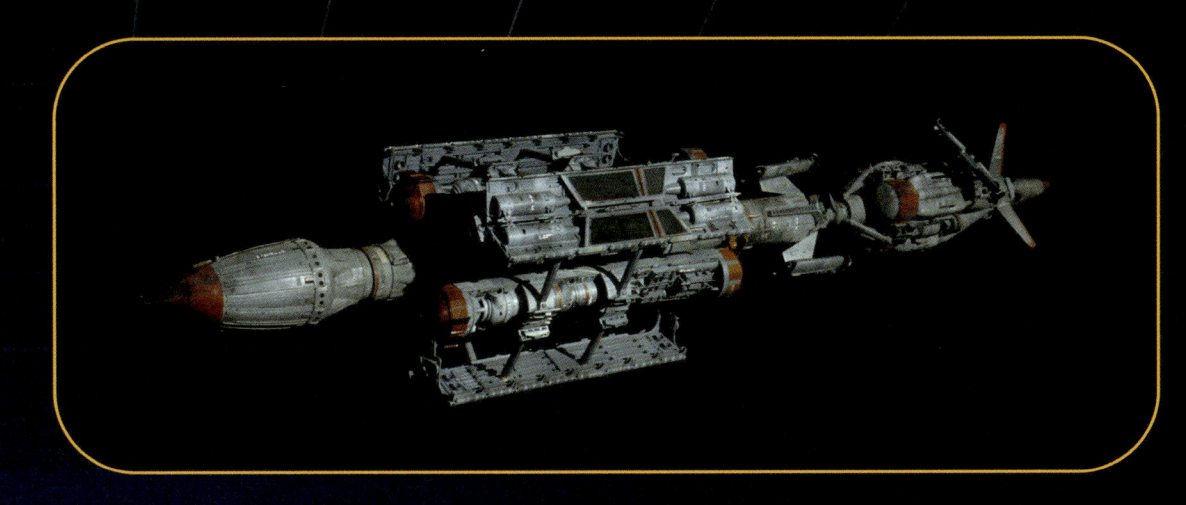

# TREEHAWK

Named for its unconventionally disguised launching platform, a giant redwood tree, Treehawk is primarily a shuttle that quickly and reliably connects Hawknest to Spacehawk.

At launch, it flies much like a conventional single-stage-to-orbit rocket, achieving orbit and docking with Spacehawk. What sets it apart is during its re-entry procedure where wings fold out from the sides of the craft allowing it to fly like a plane when in the atmosphere. Treehawk's range is not limited to Earth's atmosphere and the vehicle is able to reach the Moon and even Mars though it is faster and more efficient to be carried by Spacehawk.

The craft can carry a maximum crew of four with additional space for Zeroids. A light laser mount can be activated behind the cockpit which allows for a 360 degree of fire.

The Terrahawks operate two identical Treehawks meaning there is always one available to carry crew to Spacehawk and vice versa.

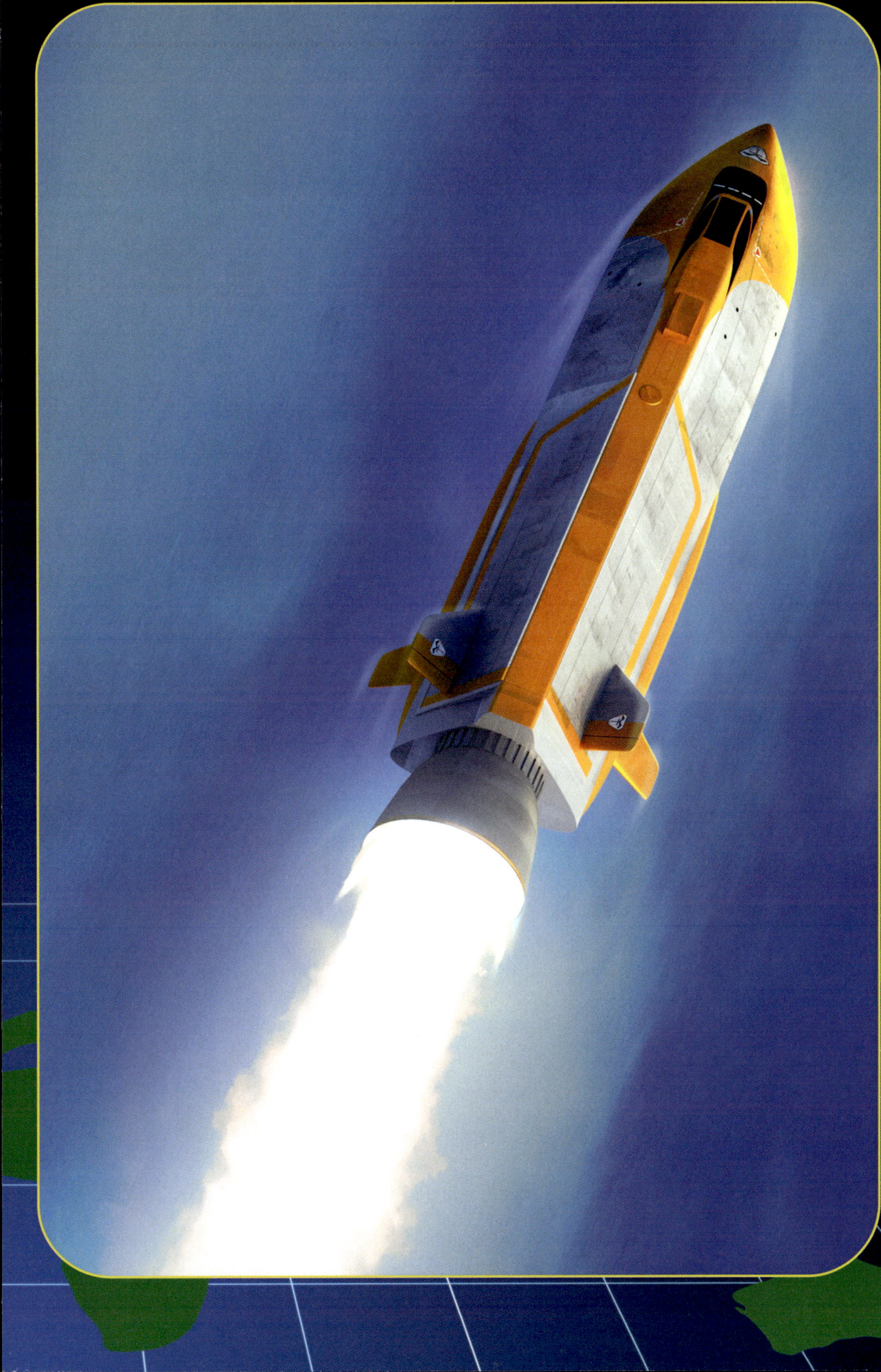

Guk's
BIG 20KG
ZERO HEALTH BENEFIT
GRANITE
CRUNCHIES
DAS IST MEINS!
OH! YUMMY!
THEY'RE WONDERFUL!
WIN!
£4.99

STAY ON THIS CHANNEL...

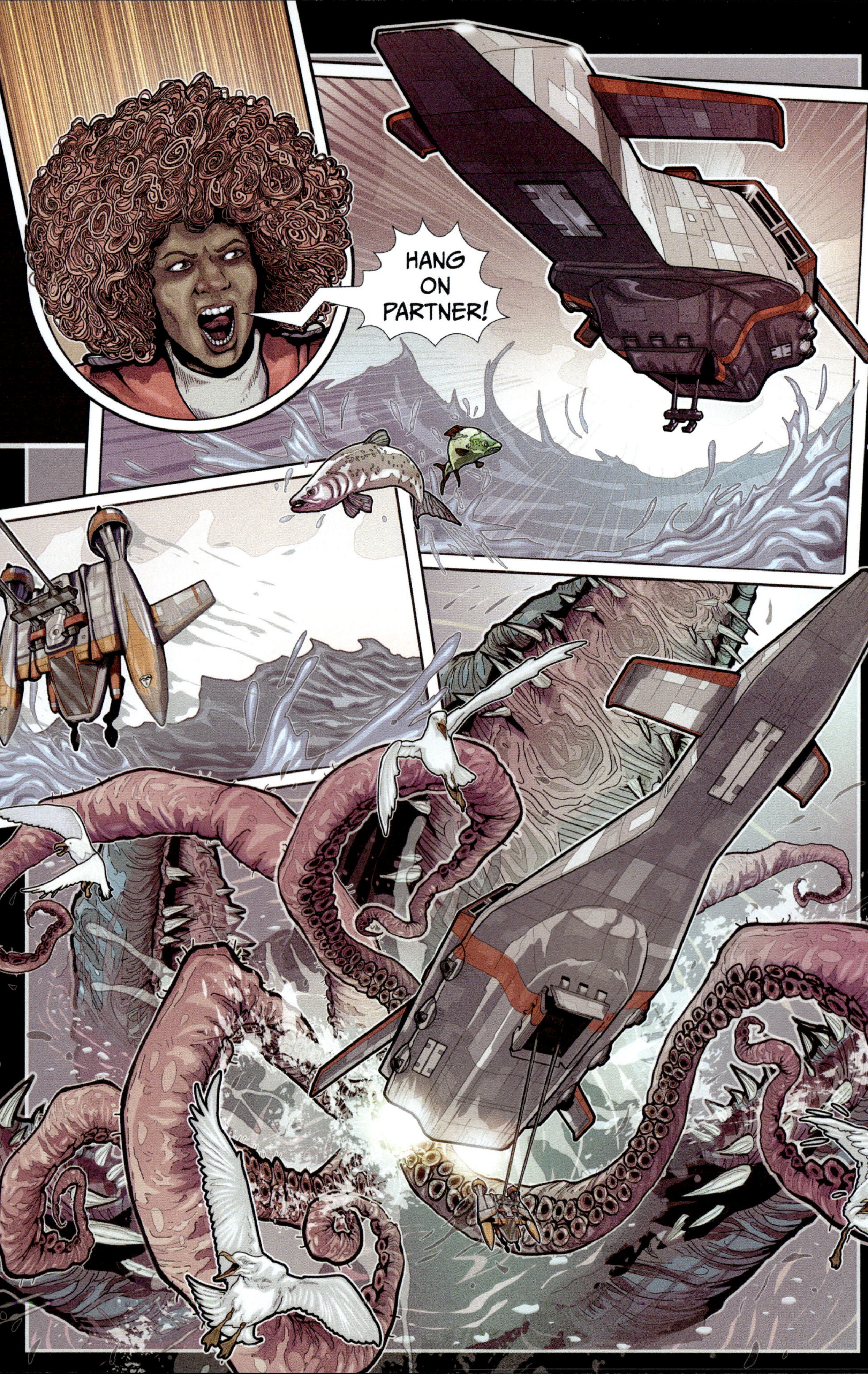
HANG ON PARTNER!

HAWKEYE!? WHAT'S YOUR 10:20?
I'M OK... I THOUGHT MY NUMBER WAS UP FOR SURE.
I ONLY SCORED ONE HIT THOUGH, THE BOMB WENT WIDE...
HIRO, HAVE WE GOT ANY MORE OF THOSE WARHEADS?
JUST ONE... I WASN'T PLANNING ON USING THEM IN THE FIELD JUST YET...
IF ONE SHOT'S ALL WE GOT THEN WE HAVE TO MAKE IT COUNT...
IN THE MEANTIME IT'S UP TO ZERO...

UGHHH, HERE WE GO AGAIN...

DEEP IN THE BELLY OF ANOTHER HARROWING CREATURE COVERED IN ENTRAILS,

THE SGT. MAJOR ZERO STORY...

ACTUALLY, THAT SOUNDS RATHER GOOD...

AAANND THERE'S THE GOOD DOCTOR.

BETTER GET A STROLL ON!

SO IT LOOKS LIKE I MIGHT NEED TO ACCELERATE MY RAMPAGE...

WHERE CAN A GIRL FIND A MASSACRE ON A NIGHT LIKE THIS?

THE CREATURE HAS CHANGED DIRECTION!
NOW HEADING DUE SOUTH!
SOUTH? WHAT'S THERE?
SHALLOWER WATERS,
THE ICELANDIC COAST,
SOME SORT OF FLOATING RESORT,
THE "HARPA MERIDIAN"...
WAIT...
THE HARPA MERIDIAN!?
THANK YOU!
THANK YOU!
THANK YOU!
THANK YOU!
YOU HAVE,
LIKE
BEEN AN INCREDIBLE AUDIENCE
YEAH?
WE'VE BEEN STEW DAPPLES AND CUSTARD!
SOS
HARPA MERIDIAN
HARPA MERIDIAN STADIUM

AND NOW THE MOMENT YOU'VE ALL BEEN WAITING FOR!
A FIRST FOR THE HARPA MERIDIAN FESTIVAL!
APPEARING VIA HOLOGRAM,
THE FANTASTIC!
THE INCREDIBLE!
KATE KESTREL!
LIFE! GOES BY SO FAST!
EVERYDAY MIRACLES COME TO PASS!
WHEN I SAID "I WISH I COULD GO", THIS ISN'T WHAT I HAD IN MIND.

I DON'T CARE IF YOUR SUPERVISOR IS AT THE CONCERT,
THIS IS AN EMERGENCY!
YOU NEED TO EVACUATE AT ONCE!
WE CAN'T WAIT FOR ZERO ANYMORE.
HIRO, WE'RE GOING TO NEED THAT TORPEDO, ASAP!
DIX-HUIT, GET DOWN THERE AND ESTABLISH A PERIMETER.
HOTEL
DIX-DIX MADAME!
ALLONSY!
18
KATE, LOOK!
THE WATER!
HARPA
83
PIER 83
PETE'S FOR EATS

K-20
HARPA MERIDIAN FESTIVAL 40TH ANNIVERSARY CONCERT
RANDOMISER

WHAT'S HAPPENING!?
THE CREATURE MUST BE MOVING VIOLENTLY,
WITH LUCK THAT COULD BE THE TERRAHAWKS COMING IN FOR AN ATTACK.
LOOK, MARY, ODDS ARE THEY'RE USING DEADLY FORCE TO DESTROY THIS THING.
THAT MEANS THIS COULD BE THE END...
I JUST WANT YOU TO KNOW...
SGT. MAJOR!
GERONIMO!!!
GOOD TO FIND YOU IN ONE PIECE MA'AM!
WHAT'S HAPPENING ZERO?
I BELIEVE CAPTAIN KESTREL HAS ENGAGED THE CREATURE. I'M TO LEAD YOU OUT BEFORE WE DETONATE ONE OF LT. HIRO'S NEW DRILL WARHEADS.
THEN LET'S GET A MOVE ON!

HIRO, IT'S OUT OF THE WATER, THE TORPEDO WON'T WORK, CAN YOU LOAD IT ON A MISSILE?
BZZZZZZZZZT!
CHOOM!
CHOOM!
10:10!
BUT I'M GOING TO NEED A FEW MINUTES!
I THINK I CAN BUY YOU SOME TIME!
DIX-HUIT, WE NEED TO "RAZZLE DAZZLE" IT.
HERE'S WHAT I WANT YOU TO DO!

SHOOM!
SOUND STA
18
PARDON PATRON!
WHY DOES THIS ALWAYS HAPPEN TO ME!?
CALLING INTERNATIONAL RESCUE...
INTERNATIONAL RESCUE, DO YOU READ ME?
INTERNATIONAL RESCUE, COME IN PLEASE!
WE NEED HELP!
SIZE
GLOW
HOLOGRAM SIZE ADJUST

♪ I TURNED MY FACE INTO THE WIND... ♪

♪ THERE'S A RESTLESS KIND OF MOTION IN THE WAY SHE BLOWS... ♪

FLAMING THUNDERBOLTS.
FALCONER
NINESTEIN
TIGER!
IS THAT YOU?
WE'RE ALL HERE,
NOT TO INTERRUPT WHATEVER *THIS* IS BUT ANY IDEAS ON HOW WE CAN GET DOWN?
HOLD ON TO SOMETHING, WITH LUCK WE'LL HAVE IT ON ITS BACK IN A MOMENT OR SO.
HIRO! HOW'S THAT MISSILE!?
MISSILE IS ARMED WITH A 10-SECOND FUSE AND IN THE TUBE!
FIRE WHEN READY!
52
READY FOR THAT SECOND SHOT PARTNER?
SHE'S NO HAWKWING BUT GET THOSE ARMS OUT OF THE WAY AND IT WON'T BE A PROBLEM.
IN THAT CASE BATTLEHAWK'S ALL YOURS, STAND BY FOR MULTI-VECTOR STRIKE!

♪ THE LIGHTS ARE OUT ♪ ♪ IN LONDON TOWN! ♪

ALL ZEROIDS CONCENTRATE FIRE ON THE CREATURE'S EYES!

♪ COMMUNICATIONS BREAKING DOWN! ♪

CHOOM! CHOOM!

♪ AND IF THE CREATURE ♪ ♪ DOESN'T KILL... ♪

FASHOOM!

CRACKOOM!

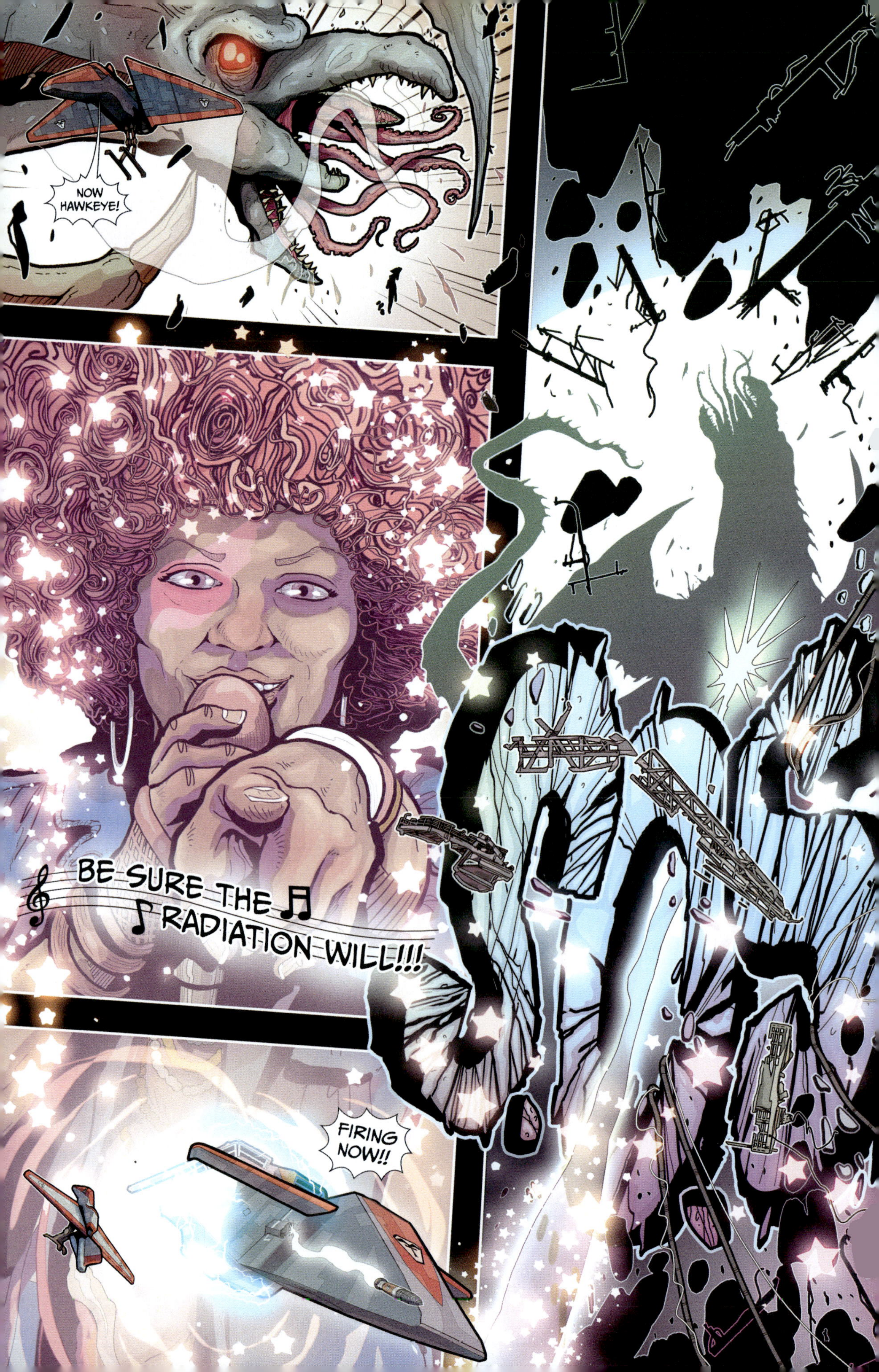
NOW HAWKEYE!
BE SURE THE RADIATION WILL!!!
FIRING NOW!!

10...9...8...

7...6...5...

4...3...2...

1...

HARPA
83
PIER 83

SUCH A SHAME...

**FAILED AGAIN MOTHER?**

**A MINOR SKIRMISH...**

**WE HAVE A WHOLE CRYOGENIC STORE OF HORRORS TO THROW AT THEM.**

UHH YEEAHH MAN, THAT WAS THE UM...

THE GLAMOROUS?

THE INCOMPARABLE?

KATE KESTREL?

**LEAVE THEM TO THEIR PATHETIC CELEBRATIONS, SOON THEIR CHEERS WILL BE REPLACED WITH SCREAMS OF AGONY.**

I DON'T SEE HOW YOU CAN BE SO CALM! BEING FOILED OVER AND OVER AGAIN BY A BAND OF FILTHY LOWLY HUMANS.

**MY IMBECILE CHILD... IF 400 YEARS OF LIFE HAS TAUGHT ME ANYTHING, IT'S PATIENCE...**

WHEN YOU'VE SLAUGHTERED YOUR WAY ACROSS THE UNIVERSE, SIMPLY KILLING YOUR OPPONENT NO LONGER HOLDS THE SAME SATISFACTION IT ONCE DID...
I WANT THE CHALLENGE.
I WANT TO STUDY MY ENEMY, SEE WHAT BRINGS THEM JOY, WHAT THEY FEAR AND SLOWLY CUT AWAY AT THEM PIECE BY PIECE.
WE MAY HAVE FAILED TODAY, BUT WE LEARNED WHERE THE REAL HEART OF THE TERRAHAWKS TRULY LIES.
AND I WON'T REST UNTIL ONE DAY I RIP THAT HEART OUT...

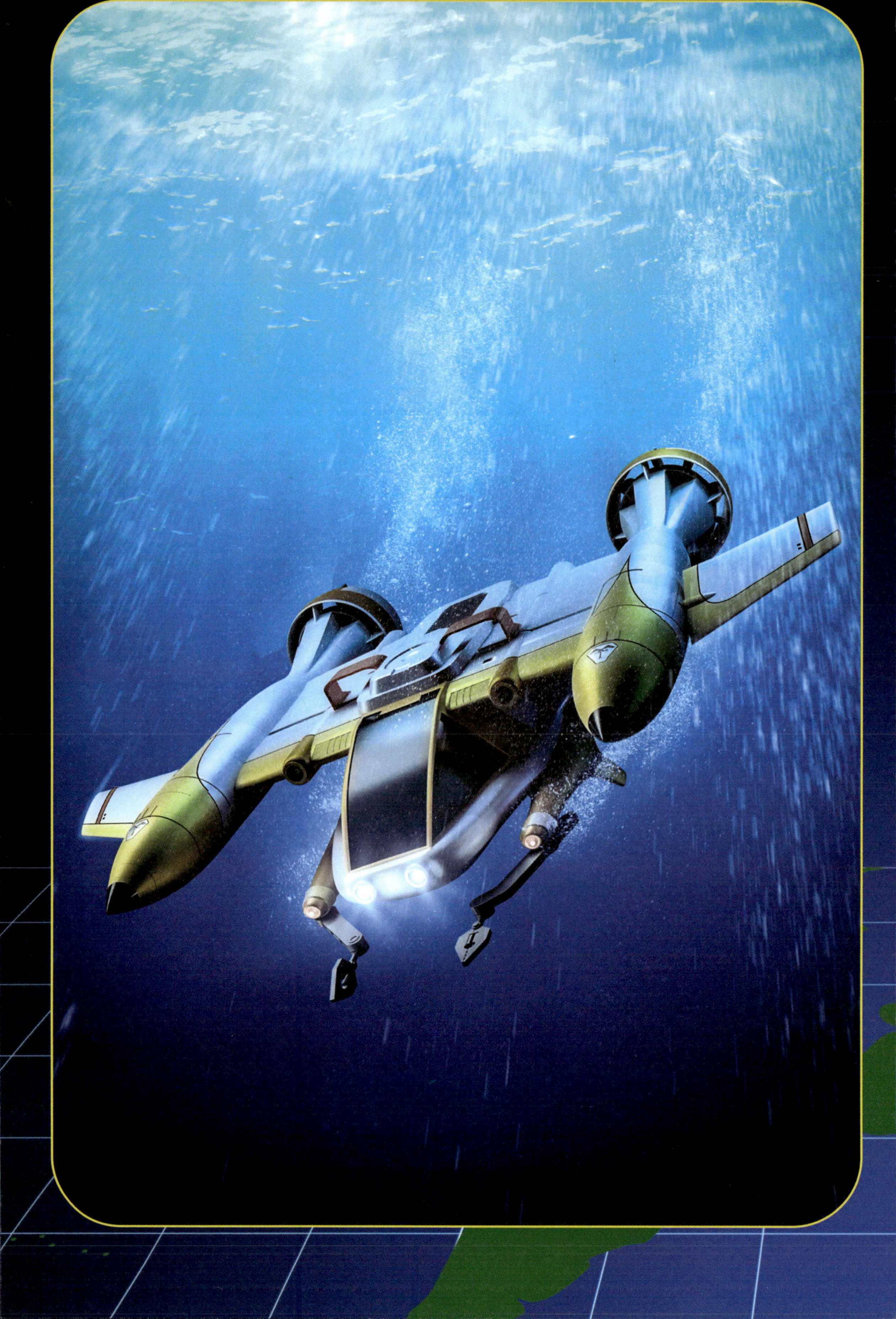

# SEAHAWK

A new and still experimental addition to the Terrahawks' fleet, Seahawk was developed to address a growing concern that the organisation didn't have a dedicated submersible and had been relying on the Zeroids to undertake any undersea missions. For this reason, an advanced deep-sea explorer vehicle was requisitioned and modified to suit the Terrahawks' purpose.

Despite being based on an existing model, Seahawk has almost wholly been redesigned from the ground up. The hull has been reinforced to sustain attack as well as being able to reach the deepest depths of the oceans. The original traditional propellor systems have been replaced by advanced turbines which give the craft an impressive speed of 60 knots while hardpoints, capable of housing mission-specific equipment or torpedoes, have been added underneath the engine nacelles.

The interior of the vessel is accessed from a ventral hatch and can accommodate two pilots with additional room for Zeroids.

Seahawk is stored at Hawknest and can be loaded into the Battletank bay on Battlehawk should the situation demand it. Similarly, it utilises a rollbar which allows it to be recovered in the same way using Battlehawks' talon recovery system.

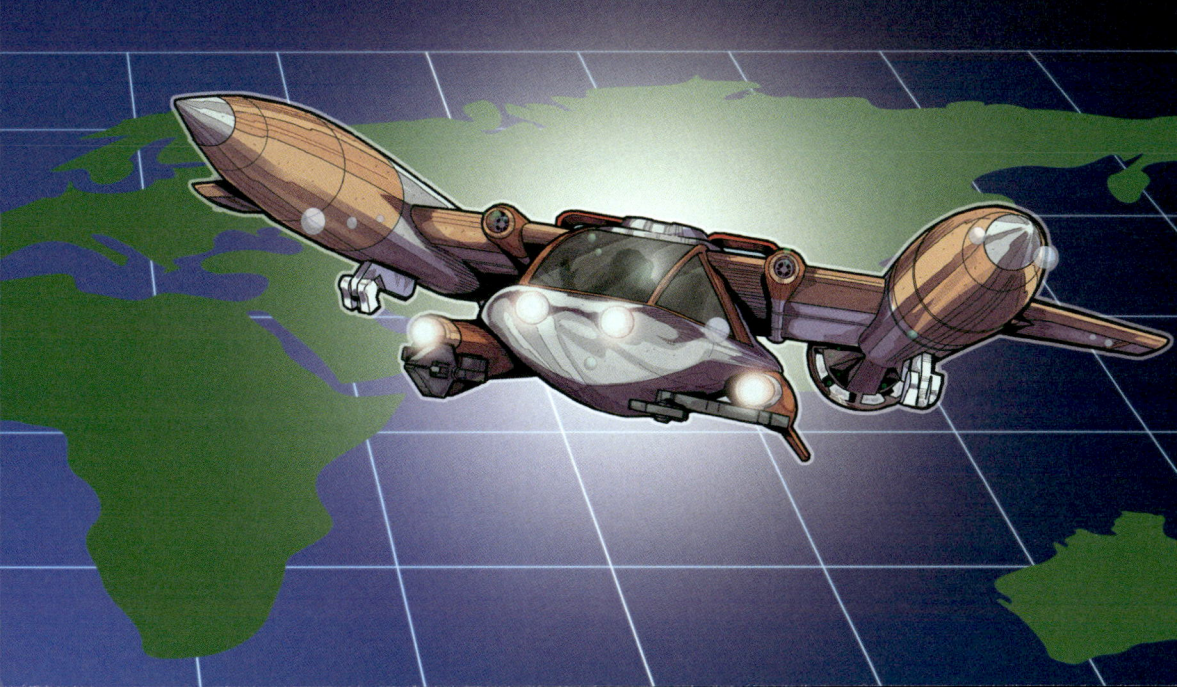

As part of an effort to buy up specialised vehicles for specific environments, the Terrahawks purchased an Arctic explorer vehicle in order to make sure they had something suitable for traversing arctic environments.

These Snowcat vehicles were specifically designed with arctic research teams in mind and would act as a mobile base with an onboard transmitter or telescope mounted on top for research purposes. A series of small living areas would also be housed onboard so that the crews could stay in the wilderness for extended periods of time.

The key design element that made these vehicles optimised for snow was the unusual tyre shape and suspension set up which displaced the weight of the craft over as wide an area as practicable while also holding the main cab as evenly as possible.

Now christened "Snowhawk" the Terrahawks' version of the vehicle retains much of the original design, the primary difference being an enhanced armour belt and a laser battery fitted to the top of the craft.

# SNOWHAWK

ANDERSON ENTERTAINMENT PRESENTS
ZERO'S METAL
A GRUDGE MATCH THAT IS OUT OF THIS WORLD!
Earth Zero
Mars Nothing!

STAY ON THIS CHANNEL...

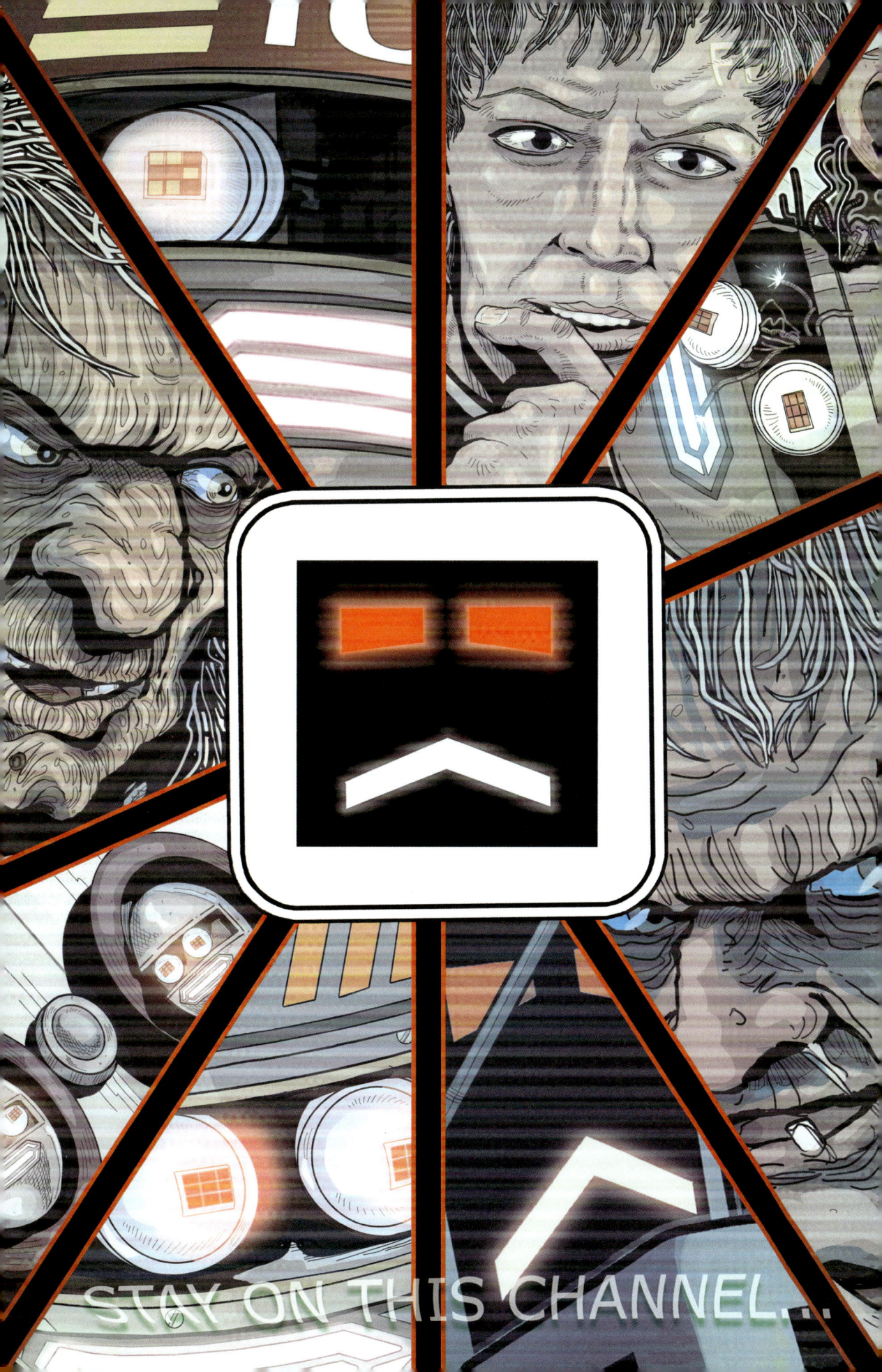

HAWKNEST, THE SECRET BASE OF THE TERRAHAWKS TEAM...

I'VE HAD ENOUGH! NO MORE EXCUSES, ZERO!

HOW MANY TIMES HAVE I TOLD YOU? ZEROIDS DON'T QUESTION – THEY FOLLOW ORDERS!

BUT DOCTOR NINESTEIN, SAH, I WAS ONLY...

NO "BUTS", ZERO! I'M SENDING YOU SOMEWHERE YOU CAN'T CAUSE ANY MORE TROUBLE –

SPACEHAWK!

BANISHED INTO ORBIT. I'LL NEVER HEAR THE END OF IT.
DON'T WORRY, SERGEANT MAJOR. THE DOCTOR KNOWS WHAT HE'S DOING. IT'LL BE NICE TO HAVE YOU WITH ME FOR COMPANY.
AND I'M SURE 101 IS LOOKING FORWARD TO SEEING YOU.
THAT'S ALL I NEED.
THAT GREAT SPACE-TWIT GLOATING...
...THIS DAY CAN'T GET ANY WORSE.

I'VE HAD ENOUGH!
NO MORE EXCUSES, YOU GURGLING HALFWIT!
YOU'RE A GOOD-FOR-NOTHING, SIMPLETON! A MECHANICAL, MORONIC FAILURE!
PLEASE, MOTHER!
GIVE ME ANOTHER CHANCE!
I WON'T FAIL YOU AGAIN!
DON'T GIVE ME PROMISES, YOU SNIVELLING WRETCH!
GIVE ME RESULTS!
EARTH SCUM
THERE!
A TRANSIT SHUTTLE RETURNING TO EARTH FROM THE MOON...

IT HAS NO WEAPONS, SO EVEN YOU SHOULD BE ABLE TO DESTROY IT!
OH THANK YOU, MOTHER!
GO NOW, YOU OBSEQUIOUS FOOL!

LEAVING??
LIEUTENANT HIRO, THIS WHOLE THING IS BEYOND MY COMPREHENSION!
IT'S ONLY FOR A FEW DAYS, SERGEANT MAJOR, AND DOCTOR NINESTEIN'S NEW ORDERS WERE VERY CLEAR.
YOU'RE IN COMMAND OF SPACEHAWK.
WHAT'S THE MATTER, ZERO? TOO BIG FOR YOU TO HANDLE?
BY ALL THE THUNDERING
DIDN'T CATCH THAT LAST PART! HAVE FUN, AND DON'T BREAK ANYTHING!
STROLL OFF YOU JUMPED-UP SPACE HOPPER.

OH GOODY! I SEE THE EARTH-SCUM'S PATHETIC SHUTTLE THING.
CUBE! OPERATE THE CAMOUFLAGE DEVICE - MAKE US LOOK LIKE THEM!
HIISSSSSSS
WHAT'S THIS?
TWO LUNAR SHUTTLES HEADING BACK FROM THE MOON. HMM...
I'D BETTER CHECK IT OUT.

ATTENTION LUNAR SHUTTLE 2, THIS IS SPACEHAWK. PLEASE CONFIRM YOUR STATUS.
OH... ERR...
WHAT DO I SAY NOW?
THIS... UMM...
THIS IS THE EARTH-SCUM...
I MEAN EARTHLING MOON SHUTTLE RETURNING TO PLANET EARTH.
FLAMIN' THUNDERBOLTS!
I'D BET MY LAST DIODE THAT'S YUNG-STAR'S VOICE - OR I'M AN OVERGROWN BALL BEARING!
THIS IS SERGEANT MAJOR ZERO CALLING ALL SPACE ZEROIDS.
DON'T LET YOUR OPTICS DECEIVE YOU, MEN. THAT'S NO MOON SHUTTLE, THAT'S A SPACE CRUISER.
PREPARE TO OPEN FIRE!
BLEEP!
WHIRRR!
CHATTER!
NOW YOU LISTEN TO ME: I KNOW YOU'RE USED TO TAKING ORDERS FROM 101,
BUT HE'S NOT HERE.
I ALSO KNOW YOU'RE THE FINEST GROUP OF SOLDIERS WHO WERE EVER PUT INTO SPACE AND YOU'RE NOT GOING TO LET ME DOWN!

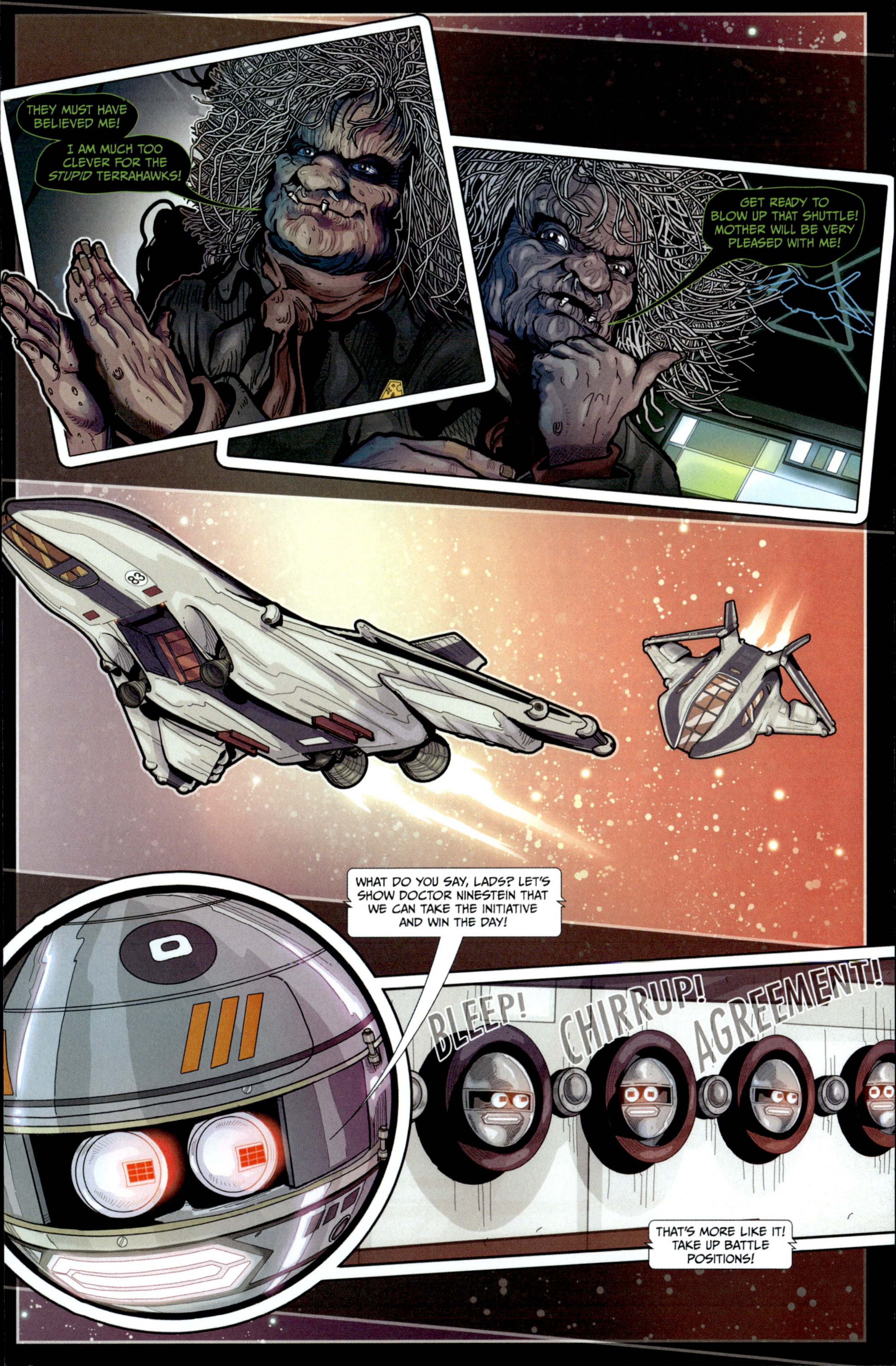
THEY MUST HAVE BELIEVED ME!
I AM MUCH TOO CLEVER FOR THE STUPID TERRAHAWKS!
GET READY TO BLOW UP THAT SHUTTLE! MOTHER WILL BE VERY PLEASED WITH ME!
WHAT DO YOU SAY, LADS? LET'S SHOW DOCTOR NINESTEIN THAT WE CAN TAKE THE INITIATIVE AND WIN THE DAY!
BLEEP!
CHIRRUP!
AGREEMENT!
THAT'S MORE LIKE IT! TAKE UP BATTLE POSITIONS!

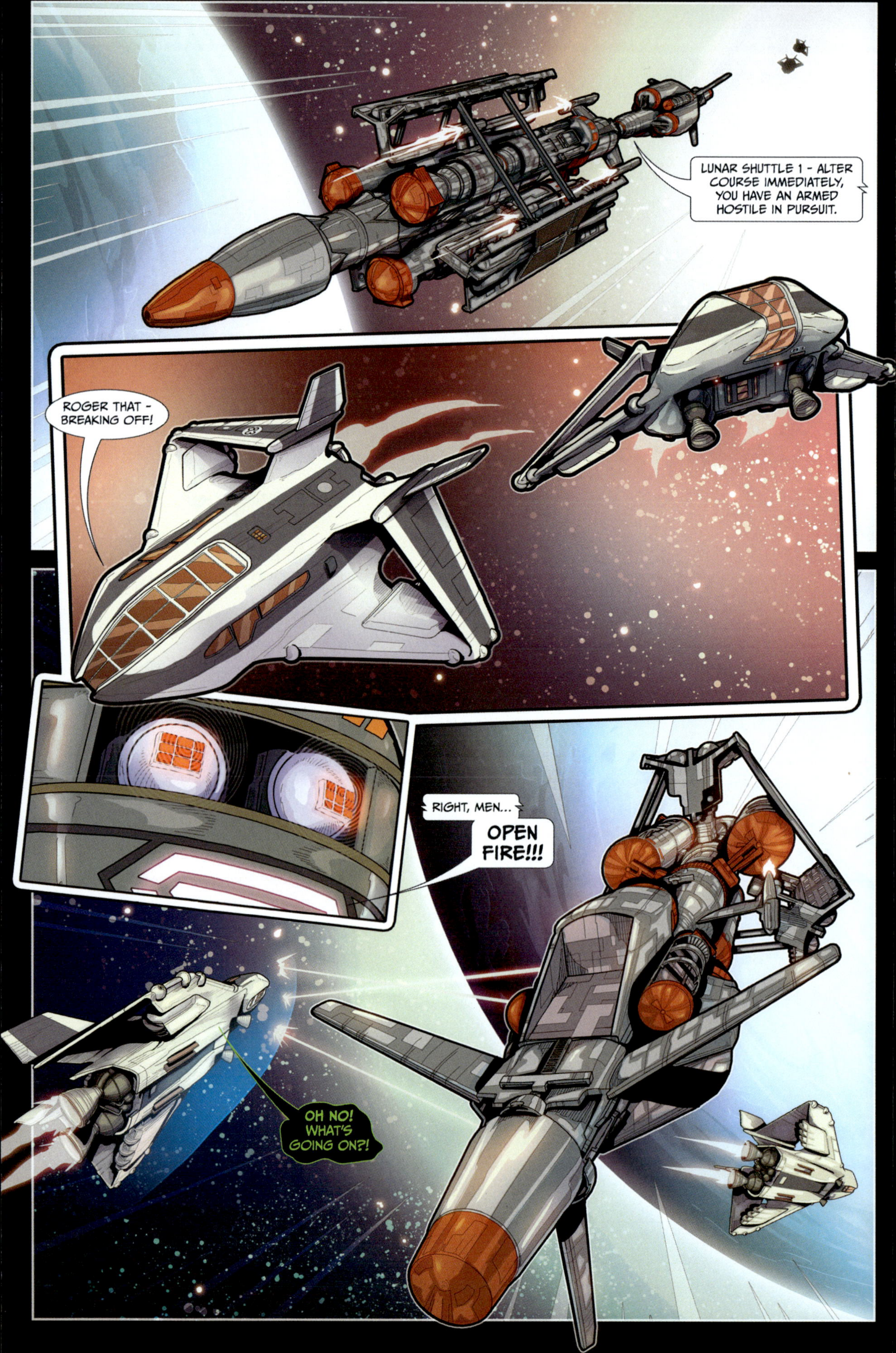
LUNAR SHUTTLE 1 - ALTER COURSE IMMEDIATELY, YOU HAVE AN ARMED HOSTILE IN PURSUIT.
ROGER THAT - BREAKING OFF!
RIGHT, MEN...
OPEN FIRE!!!
OH NO! WHAT'S GOING ON?!

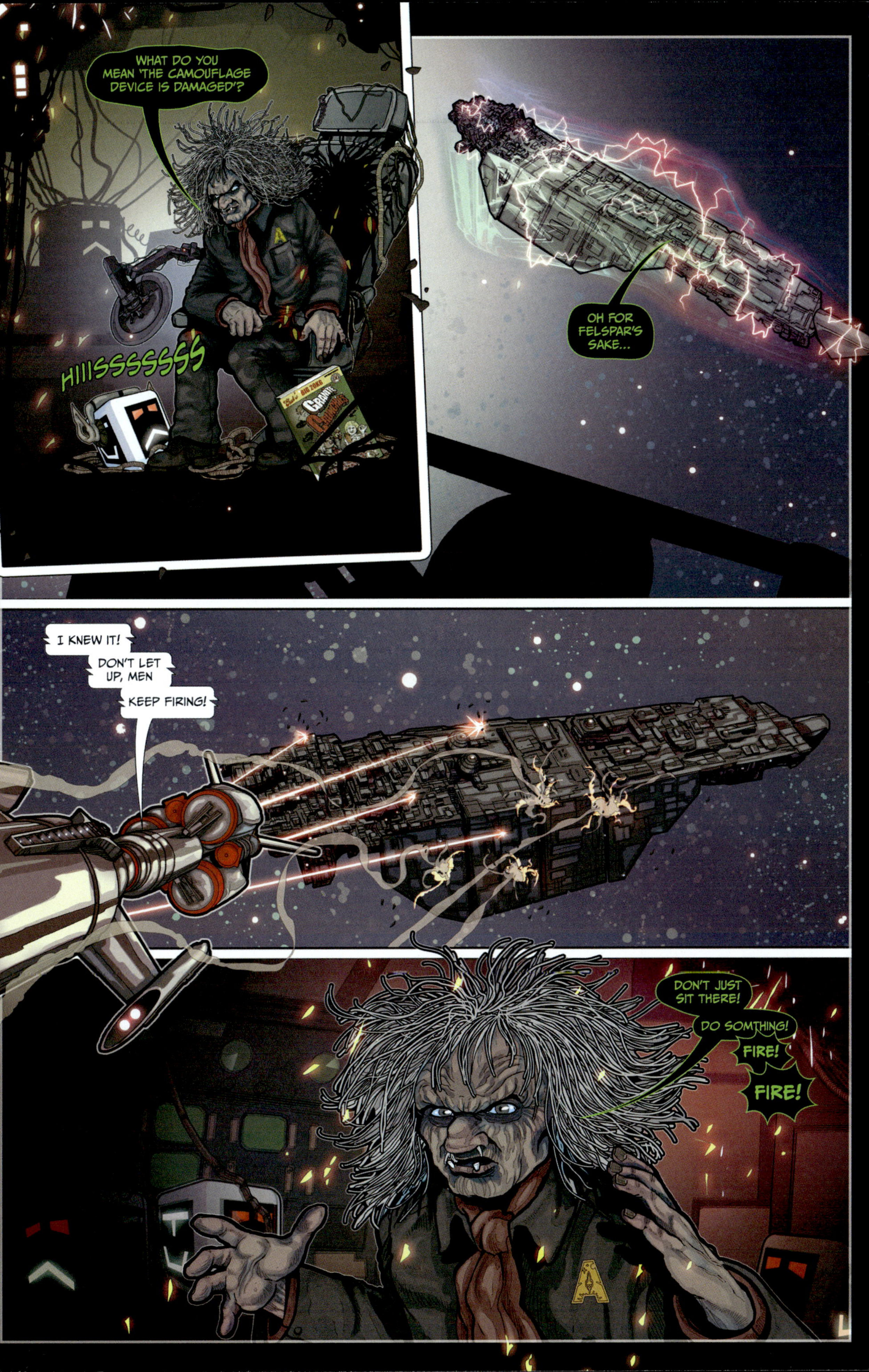
WHAT DO YOU MEAN 'THE CAMOUFLAGE DEVICE IS DAMAGED'?
HIIISSSSSSSS
OH FOR FELSPAR'S SAKE...
I KNEW IT!
DON'T LET UP, MEN
KEEP FIRING!
DON'T JUST SIT THERE!
DO SOMTHING!
FIRE!
FIRE!

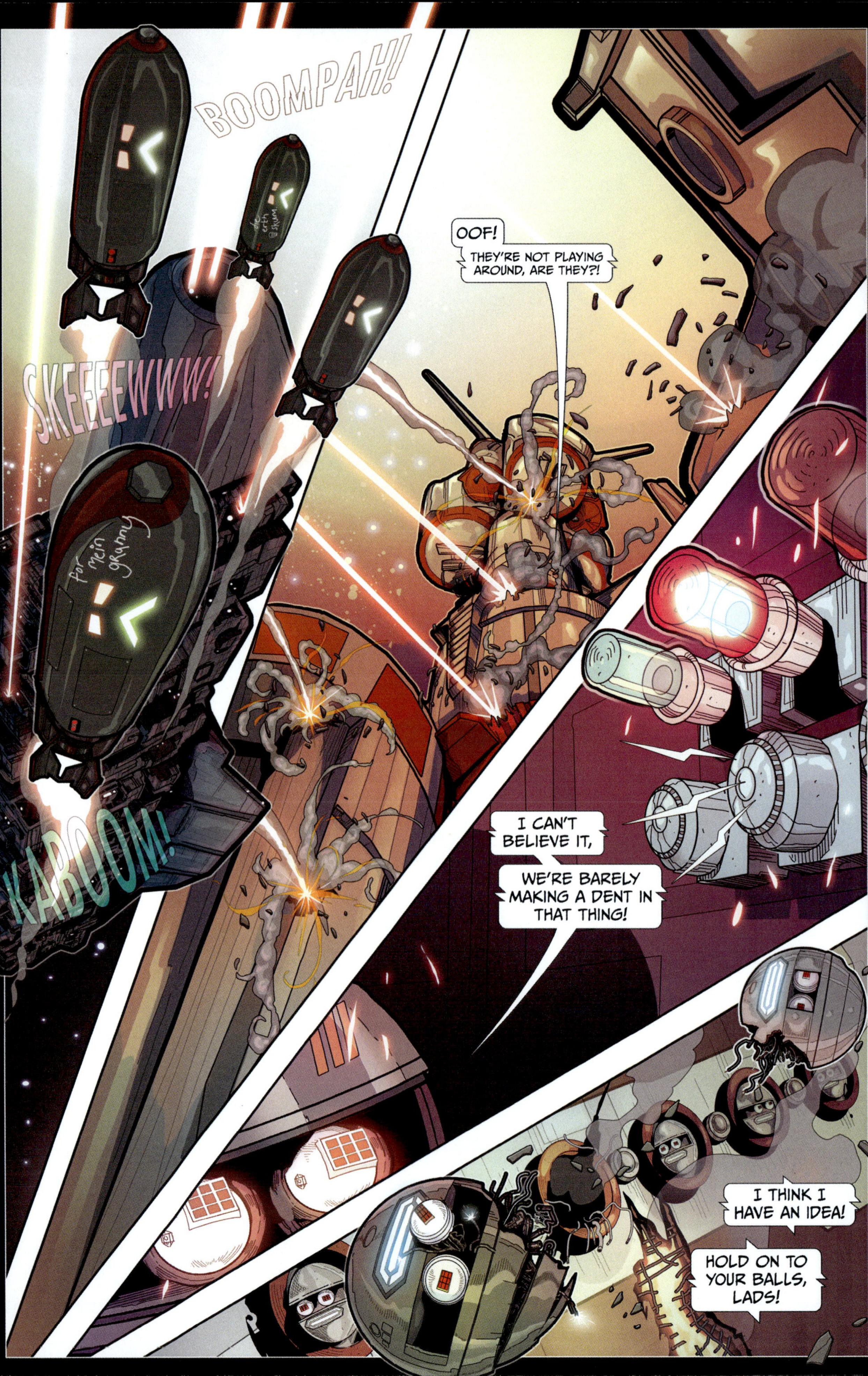
BOOMPAH!
SKEEEEWWW!
KABOOM!
OOF!
THEY'RE NOT PLAYING AROUND, ARE THEY?!
I CAN'T BELIEVE IT,
WE'RE BARELY MAKING A DENT IN THAT THING!
I THINK I HAVE AN IDEA!
HOLD ON TO YOUR BALLS, LADS!

WAIT TILL YOU SEE THE WHITES OF THEIR EYES!
WHAT ARE THE FOOLISH TERRAHAWKS DOING?
IT WILL BE MUCH EASIER TO DESTROY THEM AT CLOSE RANGE!
UGH!
THEY'RE GOING TO RAM US!
MOVE US OUT OF THE WAY!!

STEADY...
STEADY...
HOLD YOUR NERVE!
FULL POWER!
STROLL ON!
IT'S TOO LATE! THEY'LL DESTROY US ALL!
MOTHER!
SAVE US, MOTHER!
DON'T LET THEM DESTROY US!
PLEEAASSEE!!!

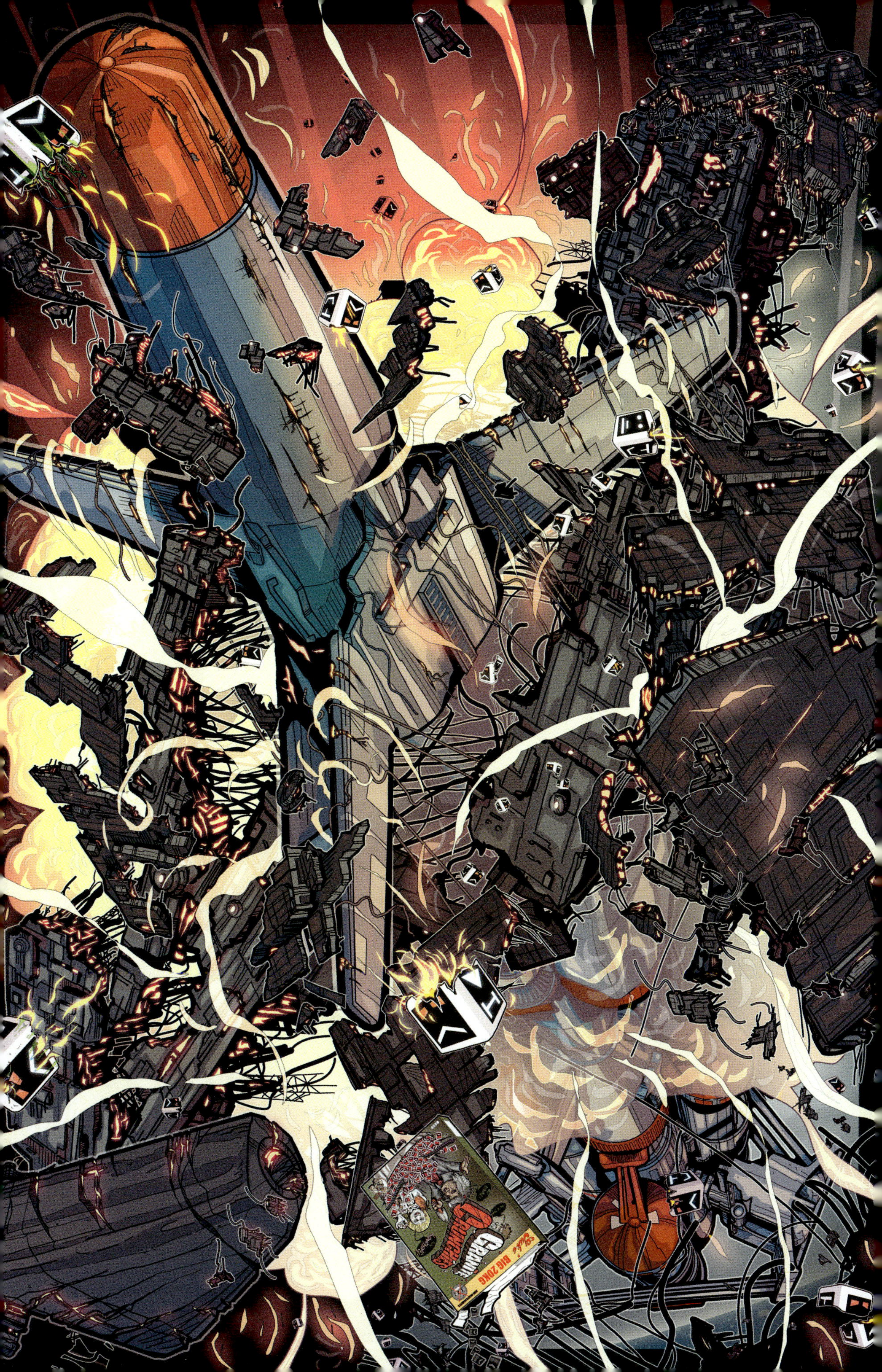
BIG ZONG

OOOOO...
I DON'T FEEL VERY GOOD...
SHOOM!
THAT'S NOTHING COMPARED TO HOW YOU'LL BE FEELING WHEN I'M DONE WITH YOU!
YOU GOOD-FOR-NOTHING, INCOMPETENT, IDIOTIC, SNIVELLING, USELESS, PATHETIC, MISERABLE EXCUSE FOR AN ANDROID!
OW!
OUCH!
I'M SORRY MOTHER!!

WELL, ZERO, I HAVE TO ADMIT YOUR ACTIONS DID SAVE THE LIVES OF THE LUNAR SHUTTLE CREW.
PERHAPS, IN THE RIGHT CIRCUMSTANCES, A CASE MIGHT BE MADE THAT OCCASIONALLY IT COULD BE BENEFICIAL FOR A ZEROID TO THINK FOR ITSELF.
THANK YOU, SAH!
PERMISSION TO RETURN TO STANDARD EARTH-DUTIES?
NOT SO FAST, ZERO.
THERE'S STILL THE SMALL MATTER OF SPACEHAWK...
HAVE YOU GOT ANYTHING TO SAY FOR YOURSELF ABOUT THAT?
I'D SAY 101 IS ABOUT TO GET THE SHOCK OF HIS LIFE...
HE...HE...HE...HE...

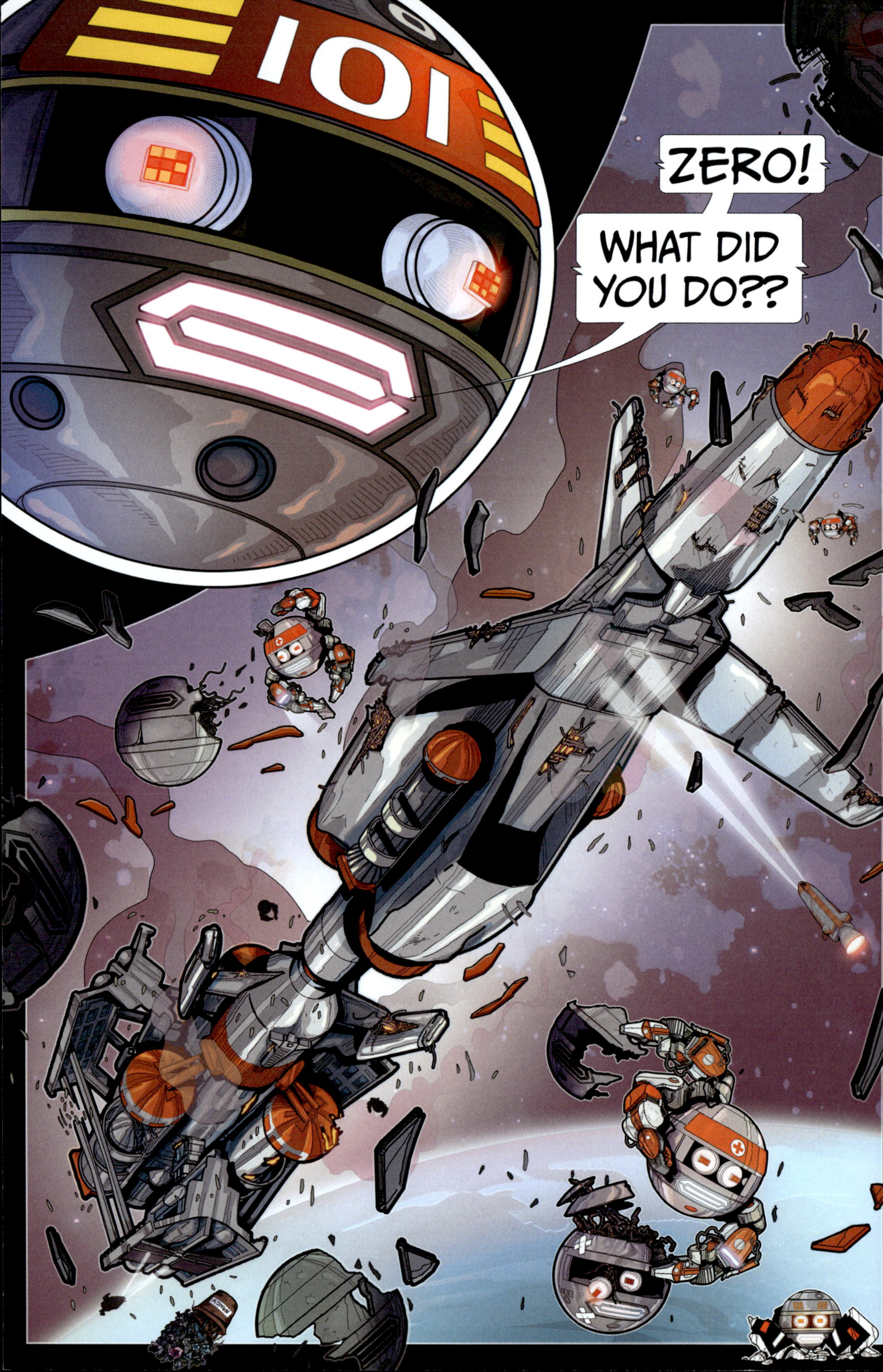
ZERO!
WHAT DID YOU DO??

ANDERBURR RECORDS

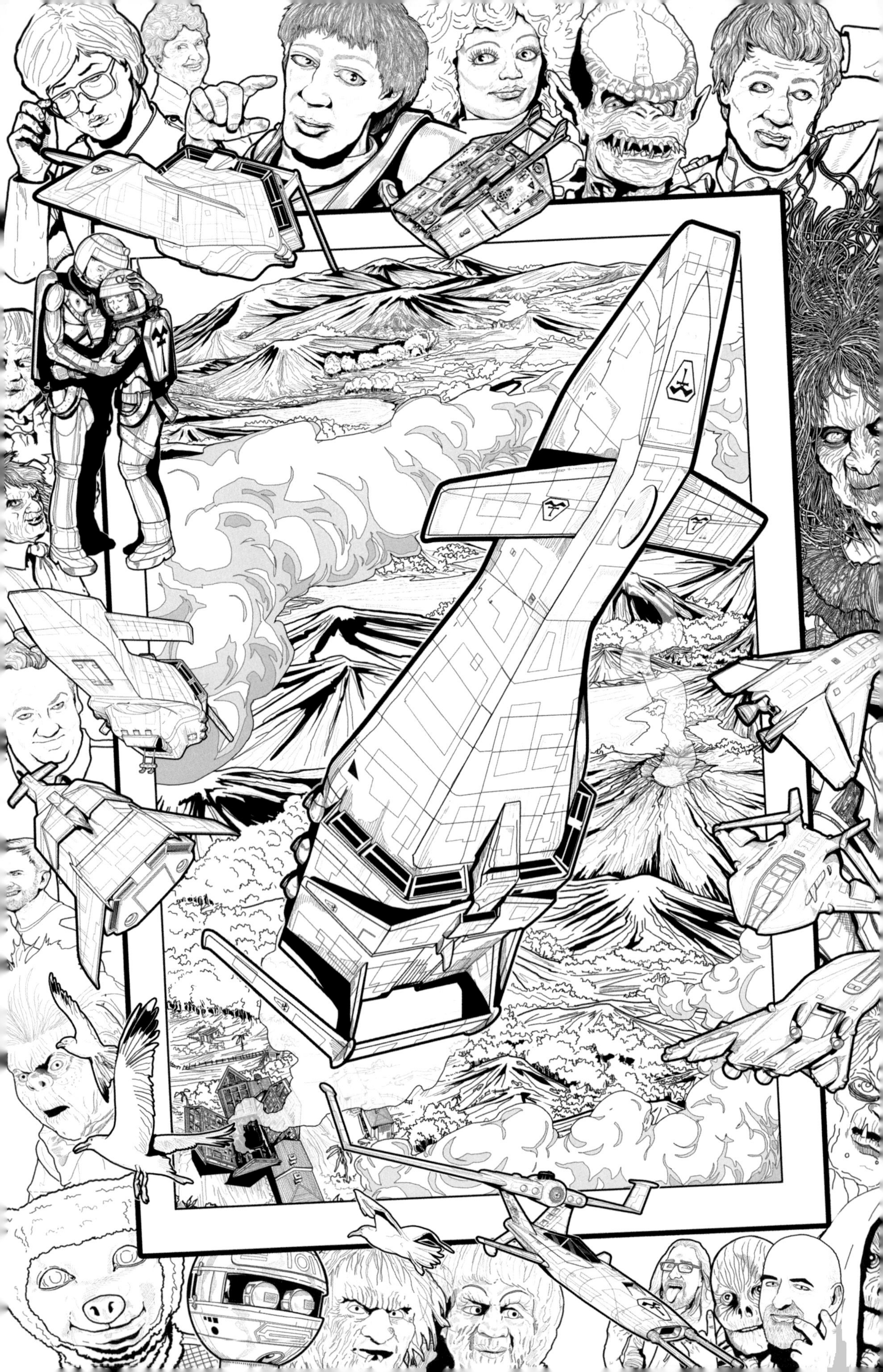

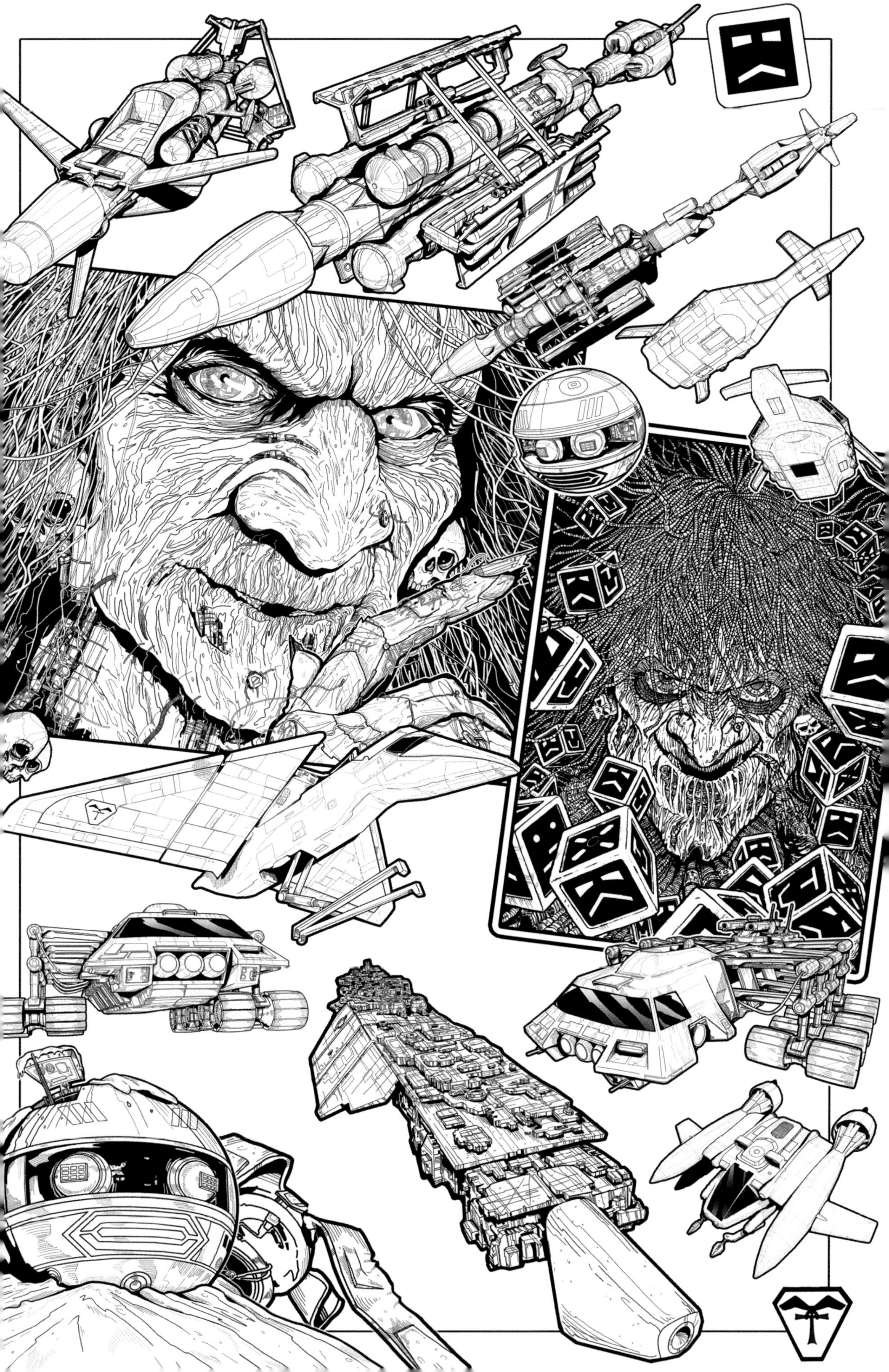

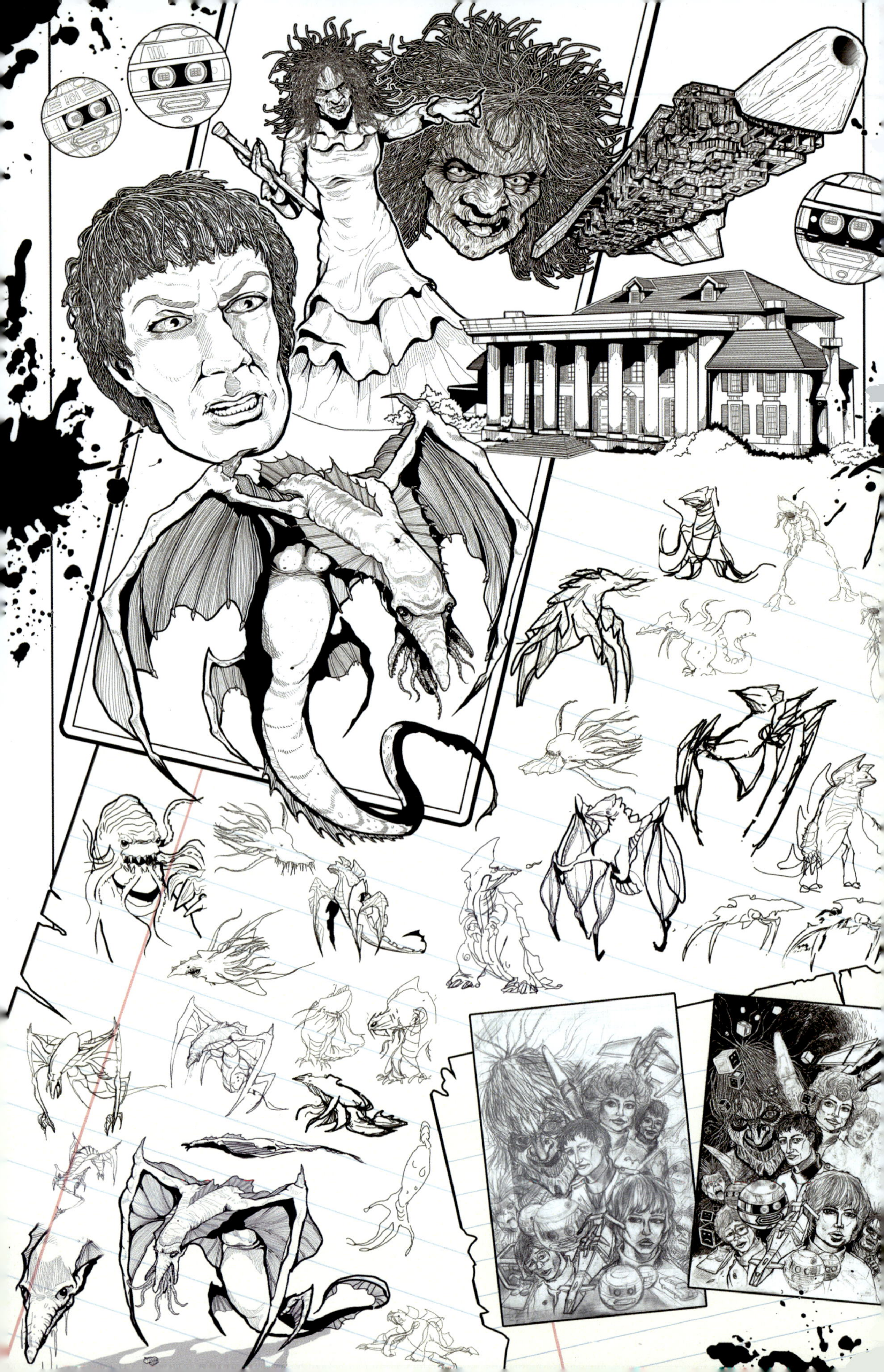

# CREATOR BIOS

## CHRIS THOMPSON — writer, Deep Blue Z.

A Belfast-based freelance creative of multiple disciplines, Chris has contributed to many Anderson Entertainment projects as an artist, writer and animator. He is probably most well known for writing and illustrating the Technical Operations Manuals on shows such as Joe 90, Space: 1999 and UFO, and producing documentary and animated features for Captain Scarlet, Joe 90, Terrahawks and Fireball XL5. Outside of Anderson Entertainment, Chris has contributed to multiple short films, music videos and several animated shorts for various Doctor Who productions.

## ANDREW CLEMENTS — writer, Zero's Metal.

AC has contributed to numerous Anderson Entertainment projects as writer, producer, director and occasional voice actor. He is perhaps best known as the creator of the web series Century 21 Tech Talk and for his continuing role as producer on Anderson Entertainment's series of Thunderbirds and Stingray audio dramas.

## CONNOR FLANAGAN — artist.

Connor is an Irish illustrator and graduate from The University of Ulster, Belfast with a BA Hons in Visual Communication, specialising in screen based imaging. He worked predominantly in the field of film and video for over a decade as both a cameraman and video editor on short films, corporate videos, equestrian events and music videos: Connor was an EPK camera operator on the movie 'Grabbers' (2012). His early art and design career involved providing illustrations for Eleven Plus practice papers, and setting design for stage productions such as The Wizard of Oz for Craic Theatre. He also redesigned the school crest for his old primary school, The Primate Dixon in Coalisland, still brandished on the uniforms of pupils some 20 years later! Connor returned to illustration in 2018 with his comic work as penciller and inker on Space Precinct: Reloaded and continues as the lead artist on Anderson Entertainment's graphic novel range.

ANDERSON ENTERTAINMENT LIMITED
THE CORNER HOUSE, 2 HIGH STREET
AYLESFORD, KENT, ME20 7BG

TERRAHAWKS: DEEP BLUE Z
SOFTCOVER EDITION PUBLISHED BY
ANDERSON ENTERTAINMENT IN 2023
ISBN: 978-1-914522-66-6

TERRAHAWKS™ AND © CHRISTOPHER BURR AND
ANDERSON ENTERTAINMENT LIMITED 1983 AND 2023. ALL RIGHTS RESERVED.

WWW.GERRYANDERSON.COM